THE GAMBLER

THE SPINSTER TAKES A GROOM

KATHLEEN LAWLESS

Cover design by Sweet'n'Spicy Designs.

ISBN ebook: 978-1-989873-61-8

ISBN print: 978-1-989873-62-5

Praise for Kathleen Lawless

ANORA'S PRIDE: "Four stars!"
~ *Heartland Critiques*

"*CALLIE'S HONOR* is a great western romance."
~ *S. Wurman, Night Owl Reviews (4.5 Stars)*

CALLIE'S HONOR: "Chemistry...steadily simmers until it finally boils over. If you have not been introduced to the works of Kathleen Lawless, this is an excellent place to start... You will not regret it."
~ *C. Bell, Long and Short Romance Reviews (4 Books)*

MADDY'S FUGITIVE "has it all—romance, action, mystery, and solid characters and plot. Tension between Jud and Maddy as well as the mystery surrounding Jud's innocence grabbed my attention and held on tight."
~ *Jen, Romancing the Book (4 Roses)*

"I liked it way too much. Lol!"
~ *Dee, Shameless Romance Reviews (4 Stars)*

MADDY'S FUGITIVE "was a fun, passionate, engaging whodunit with a strong, stubborn heroine. I was quickly drawn in ... an interesting, worthwhile story."
~ *Josie, Night Owl Reviews (4.5 Stars)*

"A fast-paced book that hooks the reader from the very first page."
~ *Anne Black, RT (4 Stars)*

～

Sign up for Kathleen's VIP Reader Newsletter to be updated on new releases or when her books go on a special fan pricing for her readers. http://eepurl.com/bVosbı

Dedication

In memory of my Dad, who I lost while I was writing this. He was always as excited as I was to celebrate every new title, and all my other writing life milestones.

PROLOGUE

Fifteen years earlier....

Selene followed her sisters and their grandfather off the train. Her oldest sister, Maia, took her and Minerva by the hand while her grandfather, Afi, scooped Chandra up in his arms. She wrinkled her nose as she looked around. The air smelled funny, different from other places they'd lived.

"This way, girls."

Selene tried to free her hand, but Maia's grip tightened. When Maia squeezed her fingers hard, Selene responded with a dig of her nails. She'd rather hold Minerva's hand. Maia was so bossy.

"There's nothing here," she said. Big, craggy mountains loomed in the distance, almost as if they were protecting the railway station. On the other side of the tracks a ribbon of a river meandered lazily past.

"There will be one day." Maia used their linked hands to brush away a chunk of hair caught in the corner of her mouth. Selene hated when she did that. "Afi is going to build a grand hotel. The grandest hotel in all the West."

Selene was unimpressed. Maia was only parroting things she heard their grandfather say.

Afi waved toward the mountains with his free hand. "Take a good look, girls. One day this will be your home." A home. Up till now they'd moved around the country from hotel to hotel, and made a game out of seeing how long their new governess lasted.

Out in the street, a man and a lady were waiting in a wagon, and took them to their house. The lady played with them while the men talked in the other room. Then the lady made them tea and bread with jam before she and her husband drove them back to the station. Afi and the man shook hands. Another train whistled its way into the station. Seated in their compartment, away from the other passengers, Selene pressed her nose to the window, unaware that five years would pass before they returned to Silver Springs Junction and made it their home.

CHAPTER 1

Selene stood on tiptoe and pushed aside several pillows to reveal a hidey hole into the study where her grandfather was pacing. Was it her imagination or did beloved Afi, as she and her sisters called him, appear more stooped this past year? He straightened at the light rap on the door, then strode across the room to open it.

"Bolton. About time."

Her grandfather's friend and confidante, who was Afi's junior by several decades, made a show of pulling his timepiece from his vest pocket. "I believe I'm actually on time to the minute."

"You're right." Afi slumped into an upholstered wingback chair as if his legs no longer had the strength to support him. "I'm an impatient old man with not much time."

Bolton took a seat nearby. "Nonsense. You're as youthful as when we first met."

"Nice try, my friend. I, too, have a looking glass."

"Youthfulness has nothing to do with appearance. It's energy and attitude."

Afi snorted. "Spoken like a man in his prime."

"I'm here now," Bolton said calmly. "What's so urgent?"

"The girls think I asked you here to track down the thief or thieves who are burglarizing guest rooms here in the hotel."

"But—" Bolton sounded as if he knew there was more to come.

"And the thieving *is* a problem. It's been happening sporadically since we first opened."

"I was not aware."

"So far, we've managed to keep it hushed. Bad for business and all that. The sheriff's not much help, and at this rate if I have to keep covering the losses out of pocket, I'll eventually go broke."

"You said there's no discernible pattern?"

"Not that I can see. But besides tracking down the responsible party or parties, I asked you here to help with a more pressing matter. The girls themselves."

Selene sucked in her breath and banged her fists together. She knew something else had to be behind Bolton's recent arrival in Silver Springs Junction.

"Your four granddaughters?" Bolton said. "They appeared in fine form when I saw them at the train station."

"What are you doing?" hissed a voice behind her.

Selene swung around. She'd been so intent on the conversation in the next room, she hadn't heard Maia. Her sister stood next to her, arms laden with freshly-ironed linens, a disapproving frown on her face.

"Sshhhh!" Selene put her finger to her lips and beckoned Maia to her side as she tuned back in to the conversation in the next room.

Afi gave his shaggy head a shake. "They're nothing like

their sweet, biddable mother. They're independent, strong-willed, stubborn—"

"Like you, you mean?" Bolton said. "Hardly surprising since you're basically the only parent they've known."

"They're of an age when they should be looking to marry. Which is where you come in. The girls were young when we first arrived. Now that they're of a marrying age, the town, while it's growing, is notably lacking appropriate suitors. I can't wait another decade. The girls are already verging on spinsterhood."

"I don't think—"

"No time for thinking," Afi said impatiently. "It's critical you get busy helping me sell the town's reputation. It needs to be more than a railway town. It needs to be a destination. One to attract the right sort of husbands for the girls."

Selene darted a glance at Maia whose face had gone as white as the linens she held. Her jaw dropped as she faced Selene.

"I'm not getting any younger, Bolt. And I'm determined to walk each one down the aisle while there's still breath in these old lungs, if I have to solicit bids from suitable candidates."

"I can't believe Afi intends to auction us off as if we were cattle," Maia whispered angrily.

"Forewarned is forearmed," Selene said as she carefully pushed the pillows back in place. "Come. We must tell the others."

"I'll find Chandra. You bring Minerva."

An easy task. Minerva could usually be found in Afi's old room next to theirs on the hotel's third floor. Once they reached their teens their grandfather had moved to the main floor, claiming the stairs were too much for his old legs to handle. Minerva had happily turned his empty room into an arts, crafts, and hobby room, largely taken over by her painting.

One far wall was lined with several worn settees, retired from the lobby. A huge table with a sewing machine at one end was littered with an array of fabric scraps, old magazines, wallpaper ends, and assorted odds and sods that eventually migrated here. On the other side, near the window with the best light, Minerva's easel stood alongside a second table strewn with palettes, paints, brushes and metal scrapers, along with various art tools no one but Minerva had a clue about.

Minerva's and Chandra's faces were sober as Maia, the eldest, recounted what she and Selene had overheard in the linen closet.

Minerva fiddled with a basket of buttons. "I had no idea Afi was so desperate to see us married off. He encourages our roles here at the hotel."

Selene looked at her sisters, the people who along with Afi, mattered most to her in this world. She remembered their parents, who'd seemed overwhelmed to have produced four daughters, but the memory had faded over time like an old newspaper. How different might their lives be if their parents hadn't perished in a housefire?

Unlikely that she'd have graduated from handling the hotel's accounts to overseeing the town's latest project, a high-class gaming hall. As to matters at hand—

"Afi considers our involvement with the hotel purely temporary," she said. "Something to do until we have households of our own to run. I don't know about the rest of you, but I intend to thwart his plans. I encourage you all to do the same."

"How?" Chandra asked.

Selene pressed her lips together. "We start by rejecting

any man he or Bolton parade past for our approval. But that tactic will only work if we stick together. Should one of us succumb, he won't rest until he has turned each of us into dutiful wives without an original thought to call our own."

"I thought Bolton was here to track down our hotel thief." This from Chandra.

"That's what Afi would have us believe. Luckily, we know better."

SELENE DASHED across the street from the nearly-finished gambling hall to the hotel. Time had gotten away, and early evening in the mountains had cooled the springtime air. That morning, Afi had announced that they were entertaining guests for dinner and he expected everyone to be on time. Tonight had been especially difficult to rip herself away.

Things at the hall were finally at the exciting stage, the culmination of over a year's work, from planning to creation. With Afi's blessing, Selene had been involved in every step, including countless sleepless nights fretting about construction delays and missing shipments. Tonight, once the glittering chandeliers she had ordered from the East were finally installed, she had pressed the power button. A moment destined to be unforgettable. The workers gasped in awe and then applauded as light flooded the main salon by way of the hotel's gas supply.

Tonight she could reassure Afi all would be ready for the hall's grand opening, right on schedule with the High Street Festival. Two events sure to attract folks from all over the country.

She did an excited little hop-skip as she took off her

cloak and hung it in the closet behind the front desk. The rise and fall of voices from the hotel's private dining room came her way, letting her know the others were already assembled. She didn't see the big deal if she was a few minutes late. The guests were likely only Bolton and Lila, who were practically family.

She quickly slipped into the compact powder room where she washed her hands and tidied her hair. No time to change. Her peacock-colored frock was decent, if not her best. Head high, she sailed into the dining room.

"Good evening, everyone. Sorry I'm late."

She ignored Afi's glower as she bent to kiss his cheek. Her sisters sent her concerned glances as she slid into the empty chair and flashed a bright smile at the table's occupants. The wine was already poured, which meant the meal was about to commence. Was she *that* late?

Slowly her gaze moved around the table. Bolton and Lila, as expected. Across from them was the mayor, seated next to a dark-haired man who'd not dined with them before. Could it be the meal wasn't a purely social occasion? Perhaps Afi had an important announcement. Her grandfather did love a dramatic moment.

"What did I miss?" she asked to fill the suddenly awkward silence. There was something unsettling in the way her sisters watched her. Did she detect a twinge of sympathy in Minerva's green eyes? Eyes remarkably similar to her own.

Afi harrumphed to display his displeasure with her tardiness. "You missed a formal introduction to Mr. Beckett Thompson."

The dark-haired man next to the mayor sent a faint, acknowledging smile her way. His dark eyes crinkled at the corners as if he knew something she didn't. Knowledge which amused him greatly.

"Miss Crawford," he said, raising his glass in acknowledgment of her presence. "Delighted you were able to join us."

Hmph. Selene took a sip of her wine. French.

Afi had provided the girls with a highly unusual education, including an introduction to fine wines, port, and scotch. The four of them had been well-versed in current affairs, along with literature, world history and mathematics. Almost as an afterthought, they'd been instructed on the details of setting a formal table, plunking out an acceptable tune on the piano, and hosting a gathering.

"It was a busy day at the hall. I left as soon as I was able." More silence.

Now she knew something was wrong. Normally her sisters would have been clamoring for more information. They might not understand her fascination with the details of construction, but they supported her fully and had shared her highs and lows this past year as the project progressed.

"Everything set for the Grand Opening?" Bolton asked.

"We will be, provided you entice the right sort of visitors. Those with deep pockets and a taste for high stakes gambling. Any projections?"

Flo, one of the hotel's many workers, slipped silently into the room with a heavy tureen of steaming soup and a stack of bowls. Afi stood and began ladling, passing the individual bowls to Flo, who placed one before each guest.

Selene noticed Bolton didn't answer her right away, but waited until everyone had been served and Flo left.

"Perhaps that's a question best answered by Beckett," Bolton said. "He'll be overseeing the gaming hall."

Selene's spoon clattered as it hit the side of her soup bowl. "I beg your pardon?" She turned wide, accusing eyes on Afi, daring him to refute Bolton's statement.

"That's right," Afi said mildly as he picked up his spoon.

Selene had difficulty swallowing as she stared into her soup bowl, her appetite suddenly gone.

"In no way does my presence mean an end to your involvement," Mr. Thompson said, as if unaware the bottom had just dropped out of her world.

The gaming hall was *hers!* Her brain child! Her passion! She'd been given free rein by Afi to nurture the undertaking from a vague idea to an impressive entity, a suitable compliment to the hotel. An asset to a town still in its infancy, and guaranteed to draw visitors from all over. She'd poured everything into seeing the place come to life. She admired it from every angle, every day. The hall stood for the one thing she wanted in life.

Power!

She narrowed her gaze on Mr. Thompson. If he thought for one second she had any intention of walking away from her ambitions, he was sorely mistaken. She raised her head and sent him a mysterious half-smile. It was a known fact one caught more flies with honey than with vinegar. And if she had her way, Mr. Thompson wouldn't be a fly in her honey for long.

THE MEAL WAS NEARLY over before she realized she'd seen Mr. Thompson before this evening, across the street. He'd been dressed in a way that she'd assumed he was one of the many parttime laborers hired by the builder.

Undercover!

Sent by Afi, if not to spy, at least to check up on her. Perhaps even report back. The realization rankled and she was so busy fuming, she failed to notice the others standing until she felt a hand on the back of her chair. As her seat slid out from the table, she rose and glared at Mr. Thompson.

The cheek!

The liberty!

As if she was incapable of sliding her own chair out. On the other hand, if he believed she was helpless—

"Thank you, Mr. Thompson."

"Please. Beckett. I insist."

She assumed her flirtiest behavior. "Such an unusual name."

"My mother's maiden name. My grandfather was pleased as he had sired no sons, only daughters."

Typical patriarchal attitude.

"There are many well-known families with only girls among the descendants." Like the March's. From *Little Women*. An inspiring story by Louisa May Alcott. Selene prided herself on emulating the noblest of the character traits from all the sisters. "Why did you not introduce yourself to me earlier, when you were at the hall? Or were you incognito at the behest of Afi?"

She caught a glint of admiration in his gaze. Unfortunately, he didn't back down.

"Very observant of you, Miss Crawford."

"You'd best make that Selene. Since it was your idea we be on a first-name basis."

"I notice you girls all call your grandfather Afi."

"Maia started it. She had a book about Vikings in which the grandfather was called Afi, so she adopted it to him. The rest of us followed."

"I'm guessing yours is not an old Viking name."

She shook her head, declining to point out the obvious. She and her sisters had each been named for a goddess, the one legacy from their mother. Selene wished she knew what sort of person mama had been. Or what she'd make of this latest situation.

CHAPTER 2

Beckett wasn't fooled by Selene's complacent and slightly flirtatious manner as she accepted his escort from the dining room. More than once, he'd admired her no-nonsense style as she clomped through the building site. If she had any idea her position was an unusual one, conferring with the building professionals involved, she didn't let on. The careful way she listened had won the confidence of the men working there; a tactic he admired and planned to incorporate into his own business dealings. Now might be a good time to start and practice.

"I'm sorry things got sprung on you like that at dinner. Crawford led me to believe you were aware I'd be running the show."

Her eyes narrowed. "Afi tends to tell people what he thinks they want to hear. It's one of his faults. A strong dislike of discord."

Which explained why Crawford hadn't said anything to Selene about Beckett's role till it was a fait accompli. And why he'd let his granddaughters make their own rules. No doubt Crawford regretted his earlier leniency, for he'd wound up with a household of women accustomed to having their own way.

"How about you, Miss Crawford? I saw no discord in your dealings with the workers on site."

"No need for discord, when things are simple. I'm fair, but I'm in charge. The last say is mine."

Beckett raised a brow. No man he knew would stand for such an attitude from his wife. But Selene wasn't anyone's wife. No doubt the workers returned home each night grateful for that fact. "I find life to be better all-around when one's dealings with others results in a pleasant situation for all parties," he said, failing to rise to the challenge in her tone. Selene was trying to find out how far she could push him. See if he was as malleable as her grandfather. "How would you see our situation resolved?"

"Easy," she said. "You return to wherever you came from and leave me to carry on as if we never met."

Beckett remained silent long enough to see her to start to fidget. "I'm afraid that's not possible," he said once her unease had grown to near agitation, which she took great pains to conceal. She might be accustomed to getting her way, but not this time.

He glanced over at Crawford, who was guiding his guests into the parlor for dessert and coffee. In private, the old man confided that he couldn't wait for his granddaughters to be some other poor sod's problem, and lamented the lack of suitors worthy of his girls.

Worthy! His jaw clenched. He might have risen to the top in his business endeavors, but Crawford's remark was a blatant reminder he'd never be free of his past.

He extended his arm to Selene. "Shall we?"

Hesitation flitted across her face before she accepted.

They had almost reached the parlor when an older

THE GAMBLER

woman swept through the hotel's main entrance. Adria Markle, a resident Beckett knew by reputation alone. A widow of indeterminate age, she occupied one of the town's original grand residences built on the heels of the hotel opening. Locals speculated wildly about what she got up to on her frequent absences from the town. Rumors, which Beckett tended to ignore, ran the gamut from a young, secret lover stashed far from Silver Springs Junction, to the widow heading East for an experimental medical treatment for some undisclosed illness.

Selene stiffened slightly, a reaction he only noticed because her arm against his grew tense.

"Adria," she said. "What brings you out so late?" Everything about her greeting looked and sounded forced.

"Your grandfather invited me to join you, but I was busy earlier. He suggested I pop by for dessert if I could make it."

"Your timing is perfect," Selene said. "They've just moved into the parlor."

Beckett would have to be blind, deaf and dumb not to notice the way Adria honed in on their linked arms, a calculating gleam in her eyes.

"I don't believe I've met your—" she paused, "—companion."

"Mr. Thompson is here at my grandfather's invitation," Selene said. She flashed him a coy smile. "We're not sure yet how long he plans to be with us."

So that's the way she planned to play.

"Mrs. Markle," he said gallantly. "I understand you're a woman of some influence in these parts. A pleasure to meet you in person."

Selene's smile faded instantly. He wondered what she had against the older woman, who preened at his compliment.

"Thank you, Mr. Thompson. No doubt we'll be seeing more of each other if you stay on." Sending one last look in their direction, the widow made her way toward the parlor.

"Something she said?" Beckett inquired mildly, once they were alone in the hotel's grand lobby. A huge multi-faceted chandelier sparkled overhead, illuminating Selene's delicate features, flawless skin and intelligent green eyes. A baby grand piano reposed in one corner atop an Indian-wool rug. Crawford had spared no expense in creating his dream destination hotel in the mountains, where several cross-country rail lines converged. Silver Springs Junction existed solely because Crawford willed it into being.

"It's nothing," Selene said dismissively. "She made a play for Afi when we were younger. She built her home here shortly after the hotel was completed and I guess he was lonely. The two of them spent some time together. It wasn't until she started talking about sending us all away to boarding school to turn us into proper ladies, that he came to his senses. They've been friendly ever since. But I've never trusted her motives."

"Crawford wouldn't be the first man in history to be swayed by a pretty face. She's still an attractive woman."

"I hear she fancies them young these days. You should throw your hat in the ring."

"Sorry," Beckett said. "I only gamble on a sure thing."

She raised a brow. "Does that include Silver Springs gambling hall?"

"It does."

SELENE RETAINED hold of Beckett's arm as they joined the others in the parlor. What was that quote she liked? Something along the lines of, "I'm not afraid of storms. I'm learning to sail my own ship." In this case the gambling hall was her ship and she wasn't about to turn the wheel over to Beckett. Not without a fight.

"Sherry?" Afi held the decanter aloft.

The men were all drinking scotch. "I believe I'll have a scotch, thank you."

Beckett's eyes crinkled at the corners in a way that was almost attractive. She pushed the thought aside. He posed a threat, even if her arm felt good linked through his. While he might be easy on the eyes, Beckett epitomized all the things she aspired to in life; things that came easy for a man. The Holy Trinity of success, money and power.

She'd quickly learned you couldn't have one without the others. Like a three-legged stool; remove one leg and the stool no longer functions.

"You *do* know why Crawford engaged my services?" Beckett said conversationally as they found a spot to stand near the fireplace, apart from the others.

"Let me guess," she drawled. "He didn't feel a woman was capable of successfully running a gambling establishment?"

Beckett laughed. "On the contrary, he sang your praises. So loudly I felt a certain amount of family prejudice was involved. He's very proud of you."

"But—" Selene asked, only slightly mollified. If that was the case, why had Afi blindsided her?

"I started my life journey as a gambler. You know nothing of the inner workings of a gaming house. Nothing of the mindset of a professional gambler. No clue what you'll be up against. It's too much for one person, let alone one person starting in total ignorance." When her eyes shot venom, he quickly qualified. "Not to imply you're ignorant.

On the contrary I can see you are very bright and learn fast. Your instincts when dealing with others are infallible."

Good thing he didn't know what her instincts were saying about him!

He leaned close and she caught a faint musky, masculine scent that sent goosebumps up the back of her neck. "Not only do I understand how a gaming hall works. I understand the mindset of a player about to win or lose everything on the roll of a die or the turn of a card. I know what prompts a man, or a woman, to take such a chance. To hunger for the next game. To feel only half alive without it."

Little did Beckett realize he'd just described her. The hunger that drove her as nothing else. The all-encompassing passion of which he spoke. Perhaps she and Beckett were more alike than she'd care to admit.

She straightened. "I know exactly what's it's like to want something with every fiber of one's being."

"I believe you do," he said. "Precisely why we will work well together."

Except she didn't want a partner.

But since one had been forced upon her, it would be prudent to learn everything she could from him. "I look forward to it."

Just then they were interrupted by her grandfather. "I must say, I'm happy to see you two getting along."

"You know I dislike surprises, Afi. But in this case, I find Mr. Thompson, I mean Beckett, one of your finer attempts to deal me a fait accompli."

"Touché!" Afi threw back his head and laughed, firelight playing with his silver hair, turning it molten gold.

Her grandfather was still a handsome man. No wonder women like Adria fluttered around.

"I wanted you to meet Beckett first. That's why I didn't

mention him earlier. I know your penchant to go off half-cocked with a bunch of preconceptions. Work yourself into an unnecessary lather."

Selene bit her bottom lip. Hard.

She. Did. No. Such. Thing.

She glanced across the room, feeling the eyes of her three sisters watching them while pretending not to. "Did the others know about Beckett beforehand?"

Afi snorted. "As if any of you four would be able to keep a secret from each other." He turned to Beckett. "One reason they are all on the way to becoming spinsters. A man has to pass muster with the entire lot. It's enough to send any sane man running."

"I don't know about that." As Beckett spoke, he stroked her forearm lightly, out of sight of Afi. "Some men can't resist a challenge."

Selene's ears perked up. So, Beckett enjoyed a challenge? She'd have to make sure she bested him every step. But subtly. In a way he didn't know it was happening.

Rather than move her arm out of his reach, she moved closer. He might be the enemy, but she'd never let him know she felt that way.

CHAPTER 3

As usual, Selene was the last one upstairs. She'd deliberately taken her time, hoping to find Minerva already asleep, but no such luck. Her sister, clad in her embroidered nightgown, sat at the dressing table brushing her long dark hair.

"I'm surprised to see you still up," Selene said, smothering a yawn. "It's late."

Minerva's eyes met hers in the looking glass. "And miss the chance to hear all about the intriguing and handsome Mr. Thompson? Hardly."

Selene plopped down onto her bed and unfastened her boots. "I find him neither intriguing nor handsome. He's too much of a know-it-all for my liking."

"You two were in quite a huddle after dinner," Minerva said. "Maia, Chandra and I all wished we were flies on the wall."

"You would have died of boredom," Selene said.

"I'm there already," Minerva said as she separated her long hair into sections and began to braid them together. "Maia runs the hotel as efficiently as any army general. She doesn't need me trailing after her." She abandoned her hair to prop her chin on her elbow and stare into the looking glass.

"I thought you were helping Bolton and Lila get things ready for the festival?"

She made a scoffing noise. "As if those two need my help."

Selene rose and crossed the room to her sister's side, taking up the abandoned task of braiding her hair. "We're quite the pair, aren't we? Feeling forced to follow society's dictates that gives top billing to the men."

"Life seemed easier when we were young. When it felt like anything was possible. That I could become a renowned artist. And you a successful business woman. Surely there's more to life than getting married and raising a passel of brats?"

Selene secured Minerva's hair with a satin ribbon. "Afi claims that would make him happy. But we all know he won't be happy unless we're happy."

Minerva swung about on the stool to face her. "Did you know Mr. Thompson is a legendary gambler? It's hard to believe he's prepared to abandon the thrill of the game in favor of working behind the scenes at the gambling hall."

"It is, isn't it?" Selene said as she traded her frock for her nightdress. "Kind of makes one wonder what he's really up to."

BACK IN HIS room hours after saying goodnight to Selene and the others, Beckett appreciated being one of those lucky people who didn't need much sleep. That trait had been a huge asset in the early years as he plied his talents in card games that stretched from one day into the next. Nowadays it was somewhat of a curse when trying to ease back into regular society. Respectable folks didn't burn the midnight oil. They were up at the crack of dawn looking fresh and rested and ready to take on the day.

Beckett regretted agreeing to stay in Crawford's hotel, for the place afforded very little privacy. Already he felt eyes upon him everywhere, monitoring his comings and goings, disapproving his nocturnal ramble through town.

Before he changed to his night attire, the muffled sound of a door closing somewhere inside the building caught his attention. In his experience, anyone creeping around a hotel in the middle of the night was up to no good. He pulled his jacket over his shirt and vest, grabbed his pistol and went to investigate.

The gaslights in the hallway had been dimmed. Shadows lurked around every corner. There were two full floors of guest rooms, while the owners' quarters where the girls lived occupied the third floor. Staff were housed out back in a separate building. He listened intently. Definitely footsteps on the grand staircase to the second floor. He rounded the corner that led to the staircase and peered into the gloom.

Was that a blur of movement near the top of the stairs? He started up two at a time, sticking to the sides where there was less chance of a creak from a loose board. He reached the second floor and looked both ways. Nothing. A muffled click cut through the silence. From which direction?

His instinct said right, so he started that way. The floral carpet muffled not only his steps, but those of whoever was ahead of him. The hallway twisted and turned, almost as if some wings were an afterthought and connected to the rest of the hotel later. A grandfather clock where one hallway intersected with another chimed the hour as he passed. Three a.m.

Maddeningly, the corridor came to an abrupt end. He glanced around perplexed. While it was difficult to make out his surroundings, it was possible one of the doorways he'd passed led not to a guest room, but to a passage or staircase. He knew some hotels installed hidden access points so the staff could move about without running into guests.

Heading back the way he'd come, he impulsively veered down a different corridor, only to collide with someone. A woman, judging from her outraged squeak and the soft curves he felt beneath her night attire as he instinctively reached to steady her.

"Unhand me," she hissed. The click of a handgun being readied echoed in the stillness before the weapon butted his midsection. He'd recognize that voice anywhere.

"Selene. It's Beckett."

Instantly, the gun was removed. As one, they moved closer to the dim light of a hallway lamp atop a table where the two corridors converged.

"What are you doing here?" she whispered angrily.

"I might ask you the same thing."

"I live here," she hissed.

Beck gave her a smug smile. "One more thing we have in common. Are you given to sleepwalking? Or did you also happen to hear something out of place a short time ago?"

She gathered her robe more tightly around her. Her hair had mostly escaped her loose braid and spilled across her shoulders like a dark curtain against the light-colored fabric. "Possibly an outside door," she said reluctantly. "Followed by stealthy footsteps on the stairs that were probably yours."

"You were on the third floor when you heard the outside door?"

She had the good grace to look sheepish. "I was in the kitchen heating some milk to help me sleep. I took the back staircase, hoping to surprise whoever was skulking around. Which was apparently you."

It could have been Selene that he first heard, but he doubted it. Selene's presence affected him, but not in a way that sent a warning signal to the hair on the back of his neck.

Her eyes narrowed in a hard look, as if she was trying to probe the inner workings of his brain. "I told you I couldn't sleep and came down for warm milk. What are you doing up?"

"I'm a night owl."

"Hmmph. I would have pegged you as something a little more predatory."

He took a step closer. Trailed one finger down the slender column of her throat. "I can be."

Her chin lifted. Her breath caught. He stared, fascinated by the rapidly beating pulse near where his finger rested. So, she wasn't as unmoved by his presence as she pretended.

"I wonder," he said, almost as if to himself. "Which is the real Selene. The bold temptress at dinner earlier, or the bashful maiden who finds herself alone with a man in the early hours?"

"Neither." Selene brushed his hand away as if it was a pesky fly. "Since I know the hotel security is in good hands, I'll say goodnight."

He caught her hand before she could move away. Pulled her tight against him and brushed his lips across hers. "Where I come from, that's the proper way to say goodnight."

She sucked in her breath. "You take liberties."

"When the opportunity presents."

Just then he heard the unmistakable sound of a third person approaching. He stepped in front of Selene.

Bolton appeared, stopping short at the sight of them.

Beckett moved closer to Selene, as if to protect her from prying eyes. He knew very little of the other man, other than he had recently arrived in town with his wife and seemed thick as thieves with Crawford.

"Sorry to interrupt," Bolton said, "but did either of you happen to see anyone on the stairs or in the hallway earlier?"

Selene didn't wait for Beckett's response, but moved toward Bolton as if he was her savior. Which, perhaps he was. One tempting taste of Selene's lips had only whet his appetite for more. He already looked forward to their next altercation.

"I was in the kitchen," she told Bolton. "I heard what sounded like an outside door. I came to investigate and ran into Beckett, who had also been disturbed by sounds of someone moving about the hotel."

"But neither of you saw, anything?" Bolton said.

"Afraid not," Beckett said, as Selene shook her head.

Bolton glanced out a nearby window. "It'll be light soon. Time enough to talk to the other occupants of the hotel and see if anyone else heard anything. Or reports anything missing."

"You think the jewel thief is at it again? Afi is encouraging the guests to have their valuables locked in the safe. I mean, that is why you're here. Isn't it?" Why did it sound as if Selene was baiting the other man? As if she knew more than she was letting on.

Beckett filed that question away. All the more reason to keep a close eye on her. A lady with secrets could prove dangerous.

ONCE BACK IN HER ROOM, Selene spent more restless hours. Every time she closed her eyes, she saw Beckett's face. His smoldering look as he stroked her arm, pulled her close, brushed her lips with his own. What might have happened if Bolton hadn't come along when he did?

Nothing, she told herself. Nothing would have happened!

She repeated this mantra as she helped herself to the breakfast foods on the sideboard in Afi's suite. Normally he and the girls checked in each morning before going in their different directions.

"I hear there was some excitement late last night." Afi put aside his paper as she took a seat across from him.

"Nothing I'd call exciting," Selene said as she buttered a slice of toast.

"I'd say nearly catching a thief red-handed counts as excitement," Afi said. "You were in the kitchen. Someone made a noise to send you to a different room so they could make their escape out the kitchen door."

"How do you know all that?"

"Bolton checked the doors after he ran into you and Beckett on the second floor. The outside kitchen door was ajar."

Minerva sent her a reproachful look. "You didn't tell me you had a secret tête-á-tête with Beckett last night."

"Believe me," Selene said. "It was hardly something I arranged." She glanced over at Afi. "So someone *was* here in the hotel last night who shouldn't have been. Is anything missing?"

"Not that I'm aware of," Afi said. "But if word gets out

about an intruder skulking through the place in the wee hours, it'll be bad for business."

Maia pressed her lips together. "Which is why it stays inside this room. With the festival a few weeks away, we can't have rumors circulating that would dissuade guests from staying with us."

"I hope you told that to Beckett," Selene said.

"You don't need to worry about, Beckett," Afi said mildly, picking up his paper again.

"Easy for you to say," Selene said. "He's not stomping on *your* toes, is he?"

Afi gave her a hard look. "Whether you know it or not, you need Beckett. He won't be around forever. Lose that chip on your shoulder and learn something from the man."

"Maybe that's what they were doing in the middle of the night," Chandra tittered. "Having a lesson together."

Selene lobbed her half-eaten slice of toast across the table at her sister. Chandra just grinned, picked it up and took a bite.

Selene rose and took a last sip of her tea before she set the cup down on its saucer. "I'll leave you lot to your idle gossip. I have things to do."

"Lessons to learn," Chandra called sweetly after her.

Selene resisted the urge to turn and stick out her tongue. Such an act would be childish. Even if it would bring a certain amount of satisfaction.

Muttering to herself, she crossed the lobby to the front door. Bolton got there just ahead of her and held the door. Selene thanked him curtly. She hadn't forgotten the conversation between him and her grandfather about finding suitors for her and her sisters. Maybe after seeing her with Beckett last night, he'd assume he no longer had her to worry about.

Which was worse? Bolton parading an array of suitors before her, or thinking she fancied Beckett? Each thought as despicable as the other.

Outside the hotel, she took a deep breath of crisp mountain air. Was there any place in the country more scenic than springtime in the mountains with its many varying shades of green? She passed the massive wooden standard with its huge brass bell that guarded the hotel. Another of Afi's eccentricities. It had been drummed into their heads from an early age that if the bell ever rang, they were to drop everything and run like the wind to Afi's study. To this day the bell had never sounded, and she and her sisters had long since stopped speculating as to the reason for his directive.

Inside the gambling hall, she paused to admire the impressive wooden bar that stretched half the length of the main gaming room. It had taken months to see her design come to life, but it had been worth it. Logs from nearby forests had been milled and sanded before being assembled. Sidepieces had been carved into the same intricate design as the crest on the family carriage. It was all finished with mirror panels installed behind each section. Oiled wood gleamed in the light of the newly-installed chandelier above it.

"I understand the bar was your design." She whirled. Beckett. Looking every bit as unnervingly attractive as he had last night with his shirt half-unbuttoned and his hair mussed. She forced the image from her mind. Forced herself to concentrate on the task at hand.

Workers were everywhere, assembling gaming tables at intervals around the main room. Doorways around the room's perimeter led to smaller, private rooms where more intimate games would take place. Metal grates framed in the cashiers' wickets at each end. The double-doorway in the center of the back wall led to the behind-the-scenes operations, a collection of workrooms including her office with its oversize safe.

"I'm pleased with the way it turned out." She tried to resent Beckett's presence. She really did. But Afi hadn't raised any fools. And given the short amount of time before the grand opening, she'd be foolish to rebuff Beckett's help. "I'm glad you're here."

"You mean this morning? Or generally?"

How did the man infuse those innocent words with such latent male sexuality? An implied intimacy that made her stomach do an unexpected dance. "I am looking forward to both your assistance and your tutelage," she said. "There is still a lot to be done before the grand opening."

He smiled down at her in a way that told her he knew exactly what she was up to. Appeasing him. And that he'd let her get away with it. For now.

Selene had no intention of sitting around waiting for Beckett to best her by showing off his superior knowledge about the gambling operations. Unbeknownst to anyone, she'd been busy educating herself. No one, not even Minerva, knew where she disappeared to some evenings. If Minerva suspected a secret beau, Selene let her think that. She knew her sister was miffed at her for keeping her assignation secret. Luckily, they were close enough that Minerva would cover for her absences if necessary. One day soon, she'd confide what she'd been up to.

CHAPTER 4

Bolton faced Crawford across his desk and shook his head when his friend lifted the decanter in silent question.

"I trust you don't mind if I indulge?" Crawford said, as he poured himself a measure of the amber liquor.

"As long as your doctor doesn't object," Bolton said mildly.

"Pah, doctors," Crawford said. "What do they know? That quack is only interested in keeping me alive so he can continue to fleece me for his house calls. The girls call him if they even suspect I might cough."

"They care about you. We all do. But first things first. Regarding our early morning intruder."

Afi glowered. "Who slipped through everyone's hands."

"Beckett and Selene probably scared away whoever it was."

Crawford barked out a half-laugh. "Beckett and Selene. Please don't tell me you caught them in flagrante?"

"Hardly," Bolton said. "Those two don't even like each other and I don't blame them, given the way you set them up. Each thought the gambling hall would be their project."

"No man is an island," Afi said. "I didn't build my empire alone. I had help."

"Some of whom became friends," Bolton said. "Others not. Did you ever think one of your enemies might be behind the hotel thefts?"

Crawford cackled. "Most of them are dead. The rest are senile."

"What about Preston?"

Crawford's eyes narrowed. "Who told you about Preston?"

"You did."

"Never mind him. He won't get near this town without me knowing his every move."

Bolton resisted the urge to roll his eyes. He had the utmost respect for Crawford, but like all men, his friend had his blind side.

"The other possibility is that the thefts are an inside job. Any newcomers join the staff around the time the robberies started?"

"Tom keeps track of all the workers and sees they get paid on time. I want to know when can I expect to see the festival start to set up?"

"There's lots of time," Bolton said. "It won't be like the circus coming to town, with the whole production piling off the train and setting up overnight. It'll be more gradual as performers trickle into town."

"I suppose," Crawford said. He squinted through lowered lids. "What if the entire undertaking turns out to be a huge flop?"

Bolton straightened. This was a side of Crawford he hadn't seen before. "It's not like you to sound unsure. You've never lent your name to anything that wasn't a huge success."

"I was younger then. Channeled all my pent-up anger and frustration over what happened first to Carolyn, then later to Melanie and Frank into making something of myself." He faced Bolton. "You ever think bad luck follows a man? Strikes when he has his guard down?"

"I believe a man makes his own luck. And bad luck falls on those who lie and cheat others. You're guilty of neither."

"Our actions come home to roost eventually," Crawford said, sitting down heavily as if his legs were suddenly tired. "One thing I regret is not settling those girls down sooner."

"I believe we only regret what we don't do," Bolton said. "If you'd settled down before you built your dynasty, that would have been a far greater regret."

"How'd you get so smart?" Crawford asked.

"Hanging around with the likes of you. I'm off to ask Tom about the staff."

"By the way, I like your wife. Reminds me a little of Carolyn."

"I'll pass along the compliment."

He cackled. "Just don't tell her she reminds me of my dead wife. She might think I have inappropriate designs on her."

"Lila can handle her own."

"She appears to have settled in nicely. Tell me. How does she fill her days?"

"She's embroiled in penning a novel. Something about a female sleuth."

"I like a woman who knows her own mind."

"Maybe you should forget about walking the girls down the aisle. Let them make their own choices for the future."

"Talk to me when you have unmarried daughters bordering on spinsterhood. You'll understand then."

Just then Flo interrupted them to announce that Mrs. Markle was asking to speak with Crawford. Bolton took advantage of the opportunity to say his goodbyes and leave by a different door. Crawford was like a dog with a bone when he was focused on a goal. He almost felt sorry for the girls. One thing was for sure. Luring a group of suitable young men to Silver Springs was going to be far more challenging than smoking out a jewel thief who didn't want to get caught.

BECKETT PUSHED OPEN the doorway to the saloon. The air was hazy with cigar smoke. Music from a tinny piano in one corner drowned out the muffled sounds of cards being shuffled, drinks being poured, monies being exchanged. No one paid him any mind as he studied the players at each table. Many of the seasoned gamblers he was already acquainted with. It was the newcomers that caught and held his attention, knowing this part of the world was ripe for the type of sophisticated gaming establishments he'd visited in France.

Having spent many of his formative years onboard the gambling boats plying the Mississippi, he was keen to oversee the territory's first really high-class gambling hall. This week, several roulette wheels had arrived and were being assembled in time for the hall's grand opening. He needed someone familiar with the game to operate them. Someone who'd lend a certain style to the place.

It was almost too bad the gambling hall wasn't his sole purpose for being here. As he continued to eye up any prospects at a nearby table, he jerked to attention. His gaze backed up for a second look. Surely his eyes were playing tricks. He'd never seen the young man to the left of the dealer, and yet there was something familiar—

His jaw dropped. *She wouldn't dare!*

His eyes narrowed. Apparently, she would.

The man's suit jacket Selene wore had been padded to add bulk and help disguise her female form. Her dark hair had been slicked back with pomade and somehow restrained beneath the wide-brimmed Cordoba hat that shielded most of her face. A dark pencil moustache rode her upper lip. Her dainty hands were disguised by clumsy-looking leather gloves much too large for her. Despite that, she held her cards in a way that told him this wasn't her first time. She placed a bet, her voice deep and unrecognizable. Clearly, she knew what she was doing.

His first instinct was to stride over there, rip off that stupid hat and reveal her true identity, before he hauled her out by the scruff of her neck. This was no place for a lady. But the men at the table with her wouldn't appreciate knowing they were being beaten by a woman.

He stepped backward until his back butted the wall. As he watched, his grudging admiration grew. She won a few hands, but not enough to upset the other players or turn them against her. It was obvious she was a newcomer here, *and* she was making a study of the game by observing her opponents. Casually she studied their reaction to her actions, and the end results of their moves. He'd also bet his bottom dollar she was counting cards.

He turned away, pissed that her presence was an unwanted distraction. He was here to recruit workers; a handful of seasoned players whose luck was on a bit of a slide. The die-hard gamblers wouldn't stick around for long. Soon as they gathered a stake, they'd be off chasing their fortune. Which was fine. He only needed their help in the short term. Once word got out, men seeking work would flood the area.

As players came and went, he singled out a few prospects, arranging to meet them at the hall tomorrow. Next time he looked, Selene's chair was empty. He hoped she was on her way home. Crawford would never forgive him if something happened to his granddaughter. Specially if the old man found out Beckett knew what she was up to, but didn't intervene.

"WHAT DO you think of the roulette tables?"

Selene started at the sound of Beckett's voice, embarrassed she'd been caught wool-gathering. The three roulette tables, the first of their kind in the territory, were certain to be a draw for the upper-class gamblers. Much as she welcomed the new additions, she resented that she had Beckett to thank for seeing them grace her establishment. At least she still considered it 'her' establishment, even as she'd been forced to bow to Beckett's greater knowledge of the workings of a higher-class gambling hall. The place needed many more people to work here than she had anticipated, but somehow Beckett had hired and trained a crew that she could find no fault with. It was hard to find fault with anything he did.

"Do you play?"

"I have," he said. "I first saw roulette in France. The French use a slightly different wheel with a single zero, but the double zero has proved more popular in the US."

Of course. One more gaming tidbit she knew nothing

about. The fact that Beckett had taken up the game overseas just added to her pique.

"I thought riverboat gambling was where you made your reputation." She avoided adding 'fortune'. One day women would have the same opportunities to amass wealth that men did. She only hoped she lived long enough to see it.

"For the most part. Although, I also visited Monte Carlo. *There's* a place that took games of chance to an entirely new level. Have you been?"

She glared as she shook her head. He knew perfectly well she'd never left North American soil. Was he deliberately flaunting his worldliness in an attempt to highlight her lack?

"I've been thinking," Beckett said casually. So casually her guard immediately kicked in. Not for one second did she believe Beckett did or said anything without analyzing it long and hard. "We should pull up a deck of cards. If you're of a mind, I can show you a few rudimentary moves. I mean, once the grand opening is behind us, there's no need for you to be on site. Unless you want to be. But if you do, you should at least know how to cut and shuffle a deck."

"I should, shouldn't I?"

"How about we meet after the evening meal? In that little library at the rear of the hotel's second floor? I've never seen a single hotel guest make use of the space."

"Splendid idea." Wouldn't it be fun to beat Beckett at his own game? Pretend she had a sudden run of beginner's luck.

"'Scuse, me, Mr. Thompson." One of the workers poked his head around the corner. "Fellow outside asking for you."

"Tell him I'll be right there."

"*We'll* be right there," Selene corrected, annoyed by the way the man deferred to Beckett.

Beckett sighed loudly. "Come along if you wish. But you're ruining the surprise."

"I don't like surprises," she said stonily as she followed him across the main room.

"That's a shame." His mouth quirked up in that irritating way that meant not only was he amused; he was amused by her. "This way." He started across the street toward the hotel, stopped and turned to face the gambling hall.

Selene followed suit. Her breath escaped in a huff. Delight warred with irritation as she studied the newly painted sign erected above the door. *Silver Springs Gambling Emporium*. The word 'emporium' was nothing short of brilliant, for it hinted at all sorts of treasures and delights inside.

"A tad presumptuous, don't you think," she said, holding onto her tempter. Curse him for noticing her oversight and taking care of it. "What if I also had a sign on order?"

"I checked the work orders," Beckett said. "I figured you had so much on your mind, the least I could do was take care of this little detail for you."

A sign announcing the type of business within was hardly a small detail, and she was furious with herself for overlooking one of the basic rules of business.

"I rather liked the exclusivity of folks hearing about the place then having to ask where it was, rather than brazenly announce it to the world," she said, trying desperately to back pedal.

His knowing look told her he wasn't fooled. "But you approve the name? Gambling Hall sounded far too understated, given what you created."

"You think flattery will help me overlook your high-handedness?"

He shrugged. "We're a team. I wanted to surprise you, and hoped it would be installed before the grand opening."

"Congratulations!' Back ramrod straight, she walked back inside.

"Don't forget about tonight."

"I wouldn't dream of it."

"I wish you were going with us," Minerva said, she changed the gown she'd worn at dinner for something more suitable for an outdoor June evening in the mountains. "You haven't seen anything of what's happening around town."

Selene tried to look suitably disappointed. Her sisters taking in the pre-festival excitement meant they'd be out of the hotel for her little get together with Beckett.

"Things will be different once the gambling hall is open and the festival is going strong. I'll be there to see all the acrobats and fortune tellers and lord knows what all else."

"Lila and Bolton will be disappointed you're not going with us."

"Why?" Selene said sarcastically. "Does he have some poor hapless bachelor to parade of in front of me?"

"I know you think you heard Afi and Bolton talking about finding us suitable matches, but honestly, I've not seen any evidence of it."

"At any rate," she forced herself to sound nonchalant. "Beckett has offered to school me in the game of poker. Possibly even roulette if I'm lucky."

Minerva wrinkled her nose. "I didn't think you even liked the man. I don't understand you voluntarily spending more time with him than absolutely necessary."

Selene smiled. "Don't you worry. I have a plan."

Minerva raised her brow. "I know that look. It's gotten you into more trouble than not over the years."

"But have you seen what happens to the other person?" Judging by Minerva's frown, the remark had gone totally over her head. "Have fun, sister. I expect a full report on the happenings in the old town tonight."

"The town's not old," Minerva said. "Barely ten years."

"That might be young by European standards, but it's old for the Western frontier. Lots of places that sprang up a short time ago are already ghost towns."

"You don't think that could happen here in Silver Springs?"

"Not if Afi has anything to say about it. Now run along and have a good time. Tell the others I'll join them on their next foray."

Alone finally, she chose her outfit carefully. It was one she'd had made with the gambling hall in mind; feminine, yet a tiny bit provocative. A rich red wine color edged in black lace, with a cinched waist and full skirt. Her bosom was enhanced in a subtle way, and she hoped the dress would distract Beckett to the point he had no idea what was happening when she beat him. Perhaps a slight wager might be in order? She wasn't above taking his money.

Humming to herself, she descended the stairs to the second floor and made her way to the library, tucked unobtrusively behind the rear staircase. The door was ajar, a triangle of golden light spilling into the hall. Her heart gave a ridiculous hiccup as she pushed it open and stepped inside.

On the far wall, the coal fireplace glowed in the otherwise dimly lit room. A gas sconce on the wall next to the compact wooden table provided the only other illumination. Although the room, like the hotel, was only ten years old, the smell of vintage leather bindings from books much older than the building gave the impression the room had sat here, undisturbed for generations.

Beckett looked up and smiled. With his back to the fire, the gas sconce illuminated only one side of his face, which gave him a rakish, enigmatic look. One which drew her in. Dared her to look more closely. To attempt to read his intentions. Her eyes were drawn to his elegant, well-shaped hands, busy with a deck of cards which he shuffled in a careless yet confident manner. She clenched her hands in the folds of her skirt. She'd yet to touch a deck of cards without wearing gloves.

"Am I late?"

"Punctual as usual."

Did he make a habit of monitoring her comings and goings? Or was he speaking sarcastically, referring to their first meeting when she'd arrived late for supper?

She slid into the chair opposite him. His presence dominated the dark and intimate room. His lashes created sweeping shadows on his cheek. And his mouth. A shiver ran through her. Why was she suddenly noticing the fullness of his lips, the chiseled lines of his jaw?

Nothing escaped his notice. "You're not cold, I hope. I started the fire earlier, but I'm afraid the room has been unoccupied for some time."

The room didn't look unused or neglected. She'd have to compliment Maia on the housekeeping staff's efforts. "Yes, a shame, really. It's so cozy."

"Intimate even, one might say."

Her eyes flew to his, as his words echoed her recent thoughts. "Shall we start?"

"Anxious for your first lesson?"

She blinked guilelessly at him. "I realized you're right. I

should know about the games of chance being enjoyed by wealthy patrons."

"They won't all be wealthy," Beckett said. "Some will be down and out. Desperate. It's good to recognize the difference." He stacked the cards neatly and slid the pile toward her. "You always start by cutting the cards. To keep the other players honest. Ensure someone hasn't stacked the deck in their favor."

She nodded and did a deliberately clumsy cut that sent a few cards sideways. "Sorry." She smoothed the stack with both hands and slid it toward him. Handling cards was much easier without gloves.

"Try again."

She studied him from beneath lowered lids. Why did it feel like he was baiting her? She made certain her second try was moderately successful.

"Not bad."

He reached behind and pulled out a Faro board which he placed between them. "I thought we'd start with Faro since it's easier to learn."

Selene much preferred the challenges of poker or blackjack, but she kept her own counsel as Beckett went through the motions of laying down the cards. She pretended to follow his instructions, her moves slow and indecisive. She deliberately made a few errors.

Was that a smirk on his face?

"I've heard Faro is popular," she said. "But don't you expect an establishment like m—ours will attract more sophisticated players? I doubt you made your fortune or reputation on the Faro board."

She met his gaze squarely for several long, silent minutes, aware he had perfected what some called the 'poker face'. And used it only when it suited him.

Abruptly he dismantled their game. "You're right. Poker is the most difficult to learn, so maybe we should try a round or two of Blackjack, also known as twenty-one."

This time she cut the cards with more confidence. They started off with him talking her through it. She heard little of what he said as she concentrated on the cards, biding her time.

She kept her expression neutral as he turned over the Jack of spades next to the Ace. "Congratulations!"

"I take it that's good? It must be beginner's luck," she said modestly. "Dare I suggest a small wager to make things more interesting?"

"Another time, perhaps. I think that's enough for one evening."

"But I was just starting to catch on."

He reached across the table and clamped his fingers around her wrist. "Were you now?" He gave a humorless laugh. "You're very good at counting cards, I'll give you that. But luckily for you, I gave up professional gambling some years ago."

"C—counting cards? Whatever do you mean?" He retained hold of her wrist, his fingers strong and warm. Her pulse raced, fueled by his touch.

He leaned forward and thrust his face close to hers. She felt the warmth of his breath, detected the faint odor of whisky. "I know you, Selene. And all your little tricks. You thought to waltz in here tonight in a fetching gown. To bewitch me before you turned the tables and displayed your skill and knowledge with a winning hand."

"I told you," she said, worrying her bottom lip. "Beginner's luck is all."

"You might have the wool pulled over your grandfather's eyes, but not mine. I watched you play the other night at the

Wolf's Lair. Playing rather well, I might add. How did you manage the convincing disguise?"

"You were there?" How had she missed him?

"I was impressed. Not only with your skill, but with your sheer audacity." The pressure on her wrist eased as he turned her hand over and stroked the soft skin. Everything tingled from his touch, the sensation chasing up her arm.

"Did— Do you think anyone else knew I was a woman?"

"No. In fact you almost fooled me, except I've become acutely aware of your presence." His smile turned downright lascivious. "I feel things around you. Things I would not feel around a man."

She flushed. "You should not speak like that to me. It's not proper."

"I agree. And were you a proper lady, I would hold my tongue. But no proper lady goes gallivanting about at night dressed like a man. How did you achieve such a credible effect?"

"One of our former guests used to be on stage. She taught me a few things during her stay."

He released her and sat back arms folded across his chest. "For someone who dislikes surprises, you deliver a few of your own."

She straightened. "Please don't tell Afi. I know he would disapprove."

"Not only disapprove, he'd be worried sick. I was relieved to see your horse safely tucked in for the night, which meant you were as well."

"My wellbeing is not your concern."

"How can I not be concerned when I witness my partner acting in a foolhardy manner?"

She blew out an exasperated breath. "Do you have any idea why I started going out in disguise? Infiltrating a world

43

run by men. Because I needed to learn how men conduct business, including playing cards. I know Afi has been humoring me with the gambling hall. He doesn't believe I'm capable of achieving anything of note on my own, but I intend to prove him wrong. He expected I'd be content playing bookkeeper here at the hotel until someone came along and swept me off my feet before turning me into a proper wife and mother. When that didn't work, he pretended to indulge me with the gaming hall."

"Marriage and children *is* society's view of a woman's place."

"Which doesn't make it right. I believe we are on the cusp of big changes in this nation. Women already have the vote in some states. The right to own property. To make their own way."

"Such changes are difficult for someone like Crawford, who was raised to believe the fairer sex in need of protection."

Selene nodded, feeling herself deflate. "I know he feels he didn't adequately protect his own wife and daughter."

Beckett raised a brow. "If his plan was to shelter you and your sisters, it backfired."

"Which he doesn't need to know," she said sweetly, bending toward him, aware of the way his eyes dipped to her decolletage.

"I don't think it's you girls Crawford should be protecting, but any hapless man who falls prey to your charms."

His eyes continued to graze her bosoms before flitting over her features. The room suddenly felt too small. The air stifling. Making it hard to breathe. She drew a shaky breath which succeeded in drawing Beckett's gaze from her face to her person. His eyes continued to linger on the swell of her bosom, knowing in his gaze.

Did he know about the prickly rush of heat from her hardening nipples to her core? The way his eyes darkened told her he did. Told her he knew things about her body she could only guess at. That he would know where and how to touch her. How to caress her in order to elicit the most delicious sensations.

Perspiration dewed her hairline. Why hadn't she brought a fan?

"Are you all right? You look flushed."

She jumped to her feet, unable to sit still any longer. To endure his gaze and imagine it was his touch. Callused palms. Talented tongue. Knowing lips. "Stop looking at me like that."

He gave a lazy smile. Why was she staring at his mouth? "Looking at you how?"

"Like you know—things."

He rose. "I do know things. A great many things." Two leisurely steps brought him to her side. "You might bluff your way through a hand of poker. But you can't bluff your way through this."

She moistened suddenly dry lips with the tip of her tongue. A movement which seemed to fascinate him. "Th—this?"

With one bent finger beneath her chin, he tilted her face toward his. "This awareness we have of one another."

She attempted to turn away, but he kept her anchored there, eye to eye. "We have no such thing."

"I say different. I can read your 'tells' when we're together. Not unlike the 'tells' of a fellow gambler. Only yours are far more interesting." He caressed the side of her neck and she fought the urge to turn her head toward him. To taste the surface of his palm. "The way your pulse quickens. Your pupils dilate. Your breath catches and your lips

KATHLEEN LAWLESS

grow rosy, inviting my kiss." His knuckles grazed the swell of her bosom. "I can only imagine the rest. Your nipples tightening into swelling buds, begging for my touch. First my hands and then my mouth. And that is only the beginning."

She reached for what was left of her dignity. Her sanity. "I thought you were here to teach me about cards."

Beckett released her to turn and gather up the cards. "Did it occur to you that I was here to teach you about you?"

"So I can protect myself from rakes and rogues?"

"You don't need my help with that, Selene. Lord help any man who tangles with you."

"Does that include you?"

"Especially me. Lucky for both of us, I'm smart enough to keep my distance."

Her mouth curved softly. "Thank you for the most enlightening lesson." She left the room slowly, aware of his eyes on her derriere, following the exaggerated sway of her hips.

CHAPTER 5

He caught up with her at the staircase. "Promise me you won't go out again in your men's attire."

She gave him a haughty look. Very different from her provocative one, moments earlier. "Why should I make you any such promise?"

Why indeed? "What if, in exchange for your word, I agree to school you in the game of roulette?"

She swayed toward him, her a faint fragrance of roses teasing his already stimulated senses. "Is that the only game of chance you are offering as a bargaining chip?"

She tried him sorely, and she knew it.

"Tomorrow. We'll meet at the emporium."

He hoped her night was as sleepless as he knew his would be.

He was in the middle of telling the staff what to expect when the doors opened the next day, when Crawford barged in. The haughty widow Adria Markle was with him. Crawford being Crawford seemed oblivious that he was inter-rupting. He rubbed his hands together as if anticipating the next steps. "All ready for the big night?"

"We will be." Beckett looked around for Selene. Craw-ford should be asking her that question, but she'd made herself scarce after their roulette lesson. Maybe she didn't trust herself to be alone with him.

"You've done a bang-up job," Crawford said, admiring the gaming tables and roulette wheels.

"Selene gets most of the credit." She'd arrived for their lesson with a crew of cleaners from the hotel in tow. While he schooled her on the roulette wheel, the workers dusted, swept, and polished, making sure everything was perfect for tomorrow night's opening.

"Yes, I see her handiwork," Crawford said. "Fancy lights and all. We both know there's more to a successful business venture than making things look pretty."

Mrs. Markle's eyes darted about the room as if taking inventory. "What are those areas blocked off for?" She pointed to the cashier cages at each end.

"That's where the players change their money for gambling chips."

"Chips?" she said.

"Chips make it easier for the dealers and other players to see the size of the bets being placed."

"Fascinating," Mrs. Markle murmured. "Thank you for bringing me, Benjamin."

Crawford harrumphed. "You left me no choice, Adria. I could tell I'd get no peace until you'd seen the place with your own eyes."

"Will women be permitted inside while gambling is underway?" the widow asked.

"Yes, they will, Mrs. Markle. Selene wouldn't have it any other way."

"Too progressive for her own good," Crawford grumbled.

"Actually, it's smart business," Beckett said. "I never thought it was right on the riverboats to have the women relegated to strolling the deck while the gambling took place inside. By making women feel welcome, wives won't resent the time their husbands spend here. Their visit will be viewed as a night out. It should up our profits on the sale of beverages as well." He shot Crawford a look. "It was Selene's idea to offer the ladies a complimentary glass of champagne while their husbands are busy at the tables. Which reminds me. I heard recently about a couple of men back East who have developed a gambling machine."

"A machine?" Crawford's bushy brows drew together.

"I'll know more about how they work once I see one firsthand, and can gauge their popularity. But if they catch on, it would be smart to be first in the area to have one. It'll bring folks here out of curiosity, if nothing else."

"I knew it was the right move, getting you involved." Crawford clapped him approvingly on one shoulder. "Selene will come to realize it as well."

Beckett doubted that. They might have struck somewhat of a truce, but he knew she couldn't wait to see the back of him, and he didn't blame her.

"A machine that takes people's money. What will they think of next?" Crawford took his leave, with Mrs. Markle trailing in his wake.

Beckett watched his old friend hold the door for the widow. He and Crawford both knew why he was really here. While Crawford claimed getting Beckett involved in the gambling hall was an afterthought, Beckett didn't fully believe him.

Moments later Selene arrived with her three sisters. He sent them a welcoming smile while doing a quick recap in his mind. Maia, the mother hen was the eldest. She oversaw the day-to-day details at the hotel. Minerva, somewhere in the middle next to Selene, struck him as a dreamer. Selene said she spent her days on the hotel's top floor painting. Which helped explain the faraway look in her eyes.

Chandra, the youngest, wore a pouty, discontent frown. He gathered the girls had all been indulged, but their younger sister had a petulant air of one who feels short-changed. He felt a faint stirring of sympathy. It must be hard being last in line. His one brother was a few years younger than him. Years later their sister had come along. Delicate and cossetted by the entire family.

"Beckett, there you are," Selene said in the brisk, no-nonsense tone of one in charge. "We waited until Afi left with the not-so-merry widow."

"Ladies," Beckett said, nodding at each one in turn. His mother would be proud to learn he hadn't forgotten his manners. "Here for a last-minute look-see before we get mobbed tomorrow?"

Maia acted as group spokesperson. "We're all curious to see what has taken up so much of Selene's time lately."

Was it his imagination or did Selene stiffen before she responded? "I expect I'll be even busier once the hall is fully operational."

"Isn't that why Beckett's here? So you can turn your hand to more ladylike endeavors?"

"Like running a hotel?" Selene said.

Maia gave Selene a hard look. "At least it's more genteel than a gambling hall."

Ah. Antagonism between the two. Minerva seemed oblivious, slowly moving in a wide circle, taking in her surroundings with wide-eyed interest. Chandra looked bored.

"We've seen it," she said. "You promised we'd go take in the sights of the festival."

"You three run along," Selene said. "I need a word with Beckett first." Behind their backs, she pulled a face and dropped her voice so she wouldn't be overheard. "They act like I dragged them in here when it was all their idea. What did Afi want?"

"I'm not sure it was so much what Crawford wanted as the merry widow."

"I told you she tried to get her hooks into Afi years back. We all imagined the worst with her as our step-grandmother."

"The Crawford I know is smarter than that."

"That puts him in the minority, given what I've seen."

He laughed. "Who made you so cynical?"

She flashed him a knowing smile. "Afi has no idea of half the things I saw moving around the country with him when we girls were younger."

Which helped explain her prickly outer shell. Her determination to succeed on her own merits. Shame Crawford was too blind to see what type of woman he'd raised. Selene would never suffer fools gladly.

"Speaking of the others, I'd best catch up. See what all the fuss is about." She appeared to hesitate. "I don't suppose you'd like to come?"

"Are you inviting me to tag along with you and your sisters? Act as chaperone, perhaps?"

"More like run interference," Selene said.

"What kind of interference would I be expected to run?"

She appeared engrossed in pulling on her gloves. "You

can help shield us from whatever 'suitable young men' Bolton has enticed to the area to meet the spinster sisters."

"Bolton? I thought his job was to apprehend the hotel thief?"

"So Afi would have us believe. It's a cover for his nefarious plans to marry us off, come hell or high water."

Beckett burst out laughing. "You have a way of making it sound like a fate worse than death."

"The others might not be quite so horrified at the prospect of a parade of young hopefuls being imported for our perusal, but I have no intention of playing that game."

No. Selene would only play games she believed she could win.

"Lead on, Macduff."

She stopped short, head cocked, eyes keen. "I wouldn't have taken you for a fan of Shakespeare."

"There's a lot you don't know about me."

FROM ITS PERCH at the far end of High Street, the hotel stood sentry over the entire town, its imposing structure balanced by the gambling hall, its across-street companion. She often felt the hotel had a personality, watching over the family, observing goings on. She hoped it was pleased with what it saw, for the street had taken on a life of its own, a far cry from her first glimpse of the place fifteen years earlier.

Hundreds of people strolled the area, pausing to watch acrobats and other street performers. Torches and bonfires illuminated the various acts, tents, and stages that lined both sides of the street. Music spilled through the air, some from nearby saloons, some part of the entertainment. The sudden surge of excitement and energy was contagious, percolating through the air and filling her with renewed vigor. So much life. So much energy.

Approaching the longest day of the year, the evening sky remained a hazy blue, backlit by the sun slipping behind the mountains. The area was infused with the sun's lingering glow where High Street wound its way to the train station in a series of switchbacks carved into the hillside.

"Afi spoke often during this past year of his vision for the festival, but never in my wildest dreams did I imagine something of this magnitude."

"He was determined to put Silver Springs Junction on the map, and he's certainly accomplished that," Beckett said. "Unfortunately—"

"Unfortunately what?"

"Unfortunately, this sort of event also attracts undesirable elements."

She faced him. "What sort of undesirable elements?"

"Pickpockets for one. When you're in a crowd like this with a myriad of distractions, make certain you hold your reticule close. Bands of thieves are known to throw sheep or pig's blood at a potential victim. One thief steps in and offers to help. While their mark is distracted, a second thief helps himself to anything of value."

She had led a sheltered life!

Further down the street she stopped, fascinated by the antics of one man who appeared to swallow a flaming sword. Nearby, a clown bounded past performing a series of handsprings, followed by a second clown on stilts holding out a hat. Watchers-by tossed pennies his way. A young girl approached them and shyly offered Selene a flower crown.

"Oh, I couldn't possibly—"

Beckett intervened, exchanging the floral offering for a

shiny coin that made the girl's face light up with delight before she ran off.

He straightened, the floral crown looking quite ridiculous in his large, male hands. "It's a solstice tradition."

"I knew that," she said quickly.

"Do you know where the word solstice comes from?"

Reluctantly she shook her head.

"Basically, it means 'sun standing still'. Now if *you* would please stand still."

He captured her chin with the tips of his fingers and placed the crown of flowers atop her hair. His skin's warmth seeped into hers before he released her, stepped back and tilted his head.

"Most becoming, your majesty."

A heated flush crept over her cheeks. "How else do people celebrate the solstice?" It was an idle question, designed to draw his attention away from her. Because if he kept looking at her like that....

"The idea is to please the God Apollo. Fire is symbolic of praising the sun, bringing luck and warding off darkness, all in aid of a healthy harvest. Tomorrow's the official solstice. Popular activities include waterplay or sunbathing. And more bonfires, of course. A silent plea to keep the sunlight upon us."

How had he gotten so close? Suddenly he was right there, his breath stirring the wisps of hair that framed her face. Blood thundered through her veins. Their surroundings dropped away, leaving her adrift in a world that encompassed only her and Beckett. She didn't hear nearby music or laughter, only the pounding of her own heart. Or was it his?

The intensity of his gaze drew her in. His mouth hovered over hers, suspended, as if he was debating whether to kiss her. Deciding for him, she raised up on her toes to close the distance, gripping his shoulders for balance. His arms encircled her, holding her close. Safe while his mouth plundered hers.

Would any woman be truly safe with this man?

Did she even care?

Heat poured through her. Nerve endings tingled in places she'd never felt tingle before. Her grip softened to a caress, finding and kneading the strength of muscles in his shoulders and arms through the silk of his jacket. Surrendering to him. Or what he called this "thing" between them. The same "thing" she'd felt that very first night, vowing to keep her distance.

Yet here she was, kissing the only man who'd held her interest longer than a minute. A man whose touch she craved, who fired her blood and stripped away her inhibitions.

The kiss ended in a mutual sigh of surrender. Rather than release her, he raised both hands to capture her face and tilt it toward his. Their eyes met and locked. His gaze carried the same questions on the tip of her tongue. Questions that would need to wait. For—

"There you are!" Maia's voice brought her back to reality with a thud. Beckett released her immediately. "Have you two seen Chandra?"

Selene turned toward her sisters. "Chandra?"

"She was with us, then she wasn't," Maia said, with a frown. "I'm worried she may have been abducted."

Selene sent Minerva a look, seeking clarification.

"She gave us the slip on purpose," Minerva said. "She wanted to explore on her own."

"I told her it wasn't safe with so many hooligans about," Maia said. "I insisted we stay together."

"That sounds exactly like something my younger sister would pull when she felt the rest of us were being too restrictive," Beckett said.

"At least she had a big brother to look to her interests," Maia said.

"It's possible she'd seen enough and started back to the hotel," Beckett said. "Why don't you two head that way? Perhaps you'll catch sight of her up ahead. Meanwhile, Selene and I can continue in the opposite direction. If she's anywhere about, we'll find her and bring her to the hotel."

"You sound very calm," Selene said as the other two women followed Beckett's suggestion. Her lips still burned from his kiss. Might he have kissed her a second time had they not been interrupted?

"It's likely your sister simply flung off the traces and wandered away to sample life on her own. She's a grown woman, but you three treat her like she is still in short skirts."

"Maia does," Selene said.

"None the less, it's still early, with many young families about. It's unlikely any harm will befall her."

Selene stopped and stared at him. "You did that on purpose. Buying her time to explore on her own."

"Did it occur to you I might also be buying myself more time? Wanting you to myself?"

"The kiss was nice," Selene said. "But in no way changes the fact that you are not needed here. I admit your tutelage has been invaluable, but—"

"But after tomorrow, you'd prefer to see me gone. Is that it?"

She swallowed thickly. "I'm glad we understand each other."

"Selene," he said, tucking an escaped strand of hair

behind her ear. "You and I understand each other far too well."

Her eyes flew to his. Saw herself reflected in his pupils almost as if she were him and he had become her. She shivered. "We should look for Chandra."

As they moved through the crowd, Selene grew aware of more than one young woman casting an interested glance toward Beckett, and a surge of possessiveness had her tuck her hand through his arm. Let them look! Let them long.

She snuck a sideways glance. It was true he stood taller than most men they passed. And his garments were more refined than the average farmer or rancher, whose appearance spoke to a hard physical life. Beckett's most physical exertion had come from shuffling a deck of cards.

As they carried on their way and he continued to draw attention, Selene came up with a brilliant idea. A way to get Beckett out of her life once and for all. All she had to do was find a woman he was powerless to resist. Hopefully one who made her home at the other side of the country.

CHAPTER 6

S ide by side they walked to the far end of High Street where it met Crawford Court next to the station, then turned around and made their way back. No sign of Chandra. And no sign of anyone losing interest in the goings on. Afi must be in his glory, seeing his dream manifested. People from coast to coast would be talking nonstop about Silver Springs Junction.

As the sky darkened, the moon made its appearance, an icy orb suspended low in the sky. Mesmerized by its seductive glow, Selene could barely look away. "The moon is so low I feel if I were up in the mountains I could reach out and touch it."

"The Native Americans call it the 'strawberry moon' because it coincides with the best time of year to pick strawberries," Beckett said.

She gave him a disbelieving look. "You made that up."

He threw up his hands in a mock salute. "I swear! The moon is opposite the sun. With the sun at its highest point during solstice, the moon is at its lowest."

Selene turned her attention from the moon to her

companion. "You continue to be full of surprises, Mr. Thompson."

"Shame you're not a fan of surprise. And why so formal all of a sudden?" His voice lowered, stirring the hair on the nape of her neck. "I mean our lips have been intimate with each other."

"I'd rather you not bring that up," Selene said. "You didn't really think we'd find Chandra, did you?"

"I think your sister will not easily give up whatever taste of freedom she's discovered this evening."

"A man!" Selene turned to him. "You think she's with a man!"

"Is that so outside the realm of possibilities?"

"I thought the rest of us set a better example than to think she needs a man to find fulfillment."

"It's human nature to long for that which has been withheld."

Moonlight silvered his face as she studied him, wondering what he longed for. "There you go again. Another startling observation from the mouth of Beckett Thompson."

"You mean my insights into human nature? One learns a lot about others when the player across the table is gambling his future, his very existence, on the turn of the next card."

Which must be how it felt to be born with a gambler's blood in your veins. Something she'd never be able to understand, even though creating a deluxe venue for gamblers to risk all had been her driving force for over a year. For her, the gaming hall was simply a first step in her drive for power.

As they approached the hotel, Selene paused to admire her accomplishment. The emporium, washed in silver moonlight. If the hotel symbolized her grandfather's jewel in the crown, this was hers. The first of many. She gripped Beckett's arm. "Is that a light on inside?"

He frowned as he turned his gaze toward the building. "Where?"

"One of the private rooms."

"It's possible a worker missed it. I'll go in and see. You go meet up with your sisters."

"I'm going with you."

He shrugged. "Have it your way."

Selene rushed ahead of him to the emporium's front door. On impulse, she tried the knob. It turned readily in her hand. She addressed Beckett over her shoulder. "Whoever was here last neglected to lock the door."

"Let's hope it was simply an oversight."

A light left on? An unlocked door? Two oversights in one night?

She moved aside so Beckett could enter first. If she'd inserted her key just now and the door opened, she would have never known the hall had been left unlocked.

Inside, Beckett touched a switch, illuminating the room with the wonders of piped in gaslight. Such an improvement over candles and lanterns, she wondered why someone hadn't invented it sooner.

"Wait here," Beckett said, "while I check the place over. If you see or hear anything, race to the hotel and find your grandfather or Bolton. Understand?"

She opened her mouth to protest, then closed it. One of them needed to be able to fetch help if needed.

She tried to picture the scene here tomorrow, bustling with excited patrons, bartenders pouring drinks for thirsty customers. She approached the bar and admired the gleaming rows of liquor bottles and empty glasses. Everything shone. The mirror behind the glasses caught her reflection and tossed it back to her, slightly distorted. The light added a pleasing tone to her skin, rendering it almost luminescent. Her eyes looked larger than normal, her mouth redder. Or were her lips still carrying the imprint of Beckett's kiss?

As if she'd conjured his image, he appeared behind her in the mirror, his hands resting lightly on her shoulders. "Nothing appears amiss," he said. "Everything is in order. Except you, who I instructed to stay near the door."

She turned without dislodging his hands. "This place is my finest accomplishment."

"Somehow I doubt it will be the last." His hands dropped from her shoulders and she immediately missed the warmth of his touch. What was wrong with her?

"Let's lock up and get you to the hotel before your sisters send out a search party for you as well as for Chandra."

No one was around when they entered the hotel. Guests must either be out enjoying the festival's preamble, or fast asleep. Beckett accompanied her as far as the second floor. An awkward moment ensued as they said good night. For some reason, Selene felt like there should be more. Ignoring the urge to kiss his cheek or exchange a short embrace, she carried on to the third floor. Popping her head into the bedroom Chandra shared with Maia, she started at the sight of Maia and Minerva seated stiffly upon the settee.

Maia looked at the doorway behind her. "We hoped you had found Chandra, and were delivering her back safely."

"We didn't rip the town apart, but we also didn't stumble across her along the way. Beckett thinks she's simply enjoying a taste of freedom."

Maia sniffed. "It might be acceptable for a young man to sow his wild oats. But not an innocent young woman."

Selene turned and folded her arms across her chest. "Did it ever occur to any of us she might be bored? Maia, you're wrapped up in the hotel. Minerva, you have your art. I have never been happier than the day I became involved with the gambling hall. How *does* Chandra fill her days?"

Minerva and Maia exchanged a look.

"Her music?" Minerva said.

"She cares for children of our guests when parents need a break," Maia said.

"Is she passionate about either of those pursuits?"

Silence. No one knew what, if anything, held Chandra's interest.

"For heaven's sake," Selene said. "We are passionate women. Women who've been raised to speak up, encouraged to know our own minds. My guess is that Chandra is still discovering who she is and what she wants."

"So true, sister dearest."

Selene and her sisters turned to see Chandra stroll into the room as if nothing were amiss. As if it was perfectly normal for her sisters to be gathered, fully dressed, at this late hour.

Selene ran her eye over her youngest sister, who certainly looked none the worse for her adventure. Chandra's eyes were shiny, her cheeks flushed.

"Did it ever occur to you that you might have given us a few bad moments? Disappearing the way you did?" Maia said.

"Last I checked, I'm an adult in the eyes of the law. Old enough to come and go without anyone's permission."

"Chandra," Minerva said softly. "We were worried. That's all."

Chandra turned to Selene. "You didn't look worried when I spotted you in the crowd with Beckett on your arm.

The two of you were laughing and gazing at the moon, totally immersed in each other."

"Things are not always the way they appear," Selene said stonily. She ignored the speculative looks from the other two. It was obviously Chandra's intent to shift the attention from herself onto someone else. "Beckett helped me look for you, even though he was convinced you were fine."

"Wise man," Chandra said. "I'd hang onto him if I were you."

Too bad Selene was already scheming the exact opposite.

SELENE WAS HEADING DOWN to breakfast the next morning when she heard an unusual noise. It sounded like muffled scratching, coming from behind the wall. She cocked her head, and listened. Definitely scratching. Probably a rodent who'd somehow gotten inside the walls. She'd alert George, their resident jack-of-all trades handyman.

The older fellow, who had been injured years earlier in a mining accident, had shown up one day offering to do odd jobs in exchange for a place to live. She knew from doing the hotel accounts that Afi, who felt sorry for the man, let him build a small room in the basement and paid him a meagre weekly stipend to do whatever was needed around the place.

She often wondered if Afi saw shades of himself in George. Afi had been lucky in his business dealings but had he not, never mind if he'd been hurt along the way, he well could have wound up in similar circumstances. It was a sobering thought. And all the more reason for her ambitious plans. She'd learned at an early age that money ruled.

Money begot power. Power begot money. In a world where men had control of both, Selene was determined to create her own destiny, dependent on no one save herself.

As she reached the second floor, the doorway to the servants' stairs opened a crack. Someone peered into the hallway.

Selene stomped over and flung open the door. Bolton's wife, Lila, stumbled into the hall nearly knocking into her.

"What are you doing on the servants' stairway?"

Lila pushed her hair back from her face and straightened. "I heard something. I went to investigate."

"You, too?" Selene said. "I expect it was a rodent. Looking for someplace warm to build their nest."

"I don't think so," Lila said.

Selene's gaze narrowed. "Where's Bolton?"

"He's been up before dawn, busy with the festival."

"And how would he feel about you skulking around on the servants' stairway, creeping unseen from floor to floor?"

"I was hardly skulking. I was investigating. It's research for my work, if you must know."

"Your what?"

"I'm writing a series of mystery books featuring a female sleuth. This hotel is fodder for the muse, with all its hidden nooks and crannies. Not to mention the unseen thief or thieves who strike from time to time."

"I wish they'd show their faces," Selene said. "Shouldn't the sleuthing be left to Bolton? To unmask whoever is responsible for the thefts?"

Lila smiled. "I offered to help. I've read a great many murder mysteries over the years. Many murders were motivated by thieves caught in the act of making off with items of great value."

"And what does your experience suggest regarding the hotel thefts?"

"The thefts are unlikely to be random. In nearly all cases I've studied, the culprit turns out to be someone known to the victim."

"Are you saying our light-fingered hotel thief is somehow known to every person staying here? And that's how they gain access to the guests' rooms and valuables?"

"Not at all," Lila said. "The true victim is Crawford. The damage that could befall his reputation if future guests were to catch wind."

Interesting theory. One worth further thought. Selene changed the subject. "Are you planning to attend the festival while it's on?"

"I wouldn't miss it," Lila said. "Make sure you visit the fortune teller while she's here. It's uncanny, the things she knows."

"Does she know who our mystery thief is?" Selene asked.

"That I couldn't say."

Selene had no intention of visiting some charlatan to listen to her hocus-pocus, but the sisters had other ideas. She'd barely started her breakfast when the other three ambushed her.

"You must come," Minerva said, brushing aside her protestations that she still had things to do before the gambling hall's grand opening.

Beckett was no help. "Everything is looked after, Selene. Go and enjoy your time with your sisters. I'll be on hand at the hall in case I'm needed."

She glared at him. Of course he would! He'd like nothing better than to steal the place out from underneath her.

"It's important," Maia said. "Remember the pact we made when we were younger?"

Stupid pact! They'd vowed they'd always stick together, no matter what happened.

"We were children," she said, grumpy at finding herself outnumbered.

Chandra shot her a challenging look. "Perhaps Selene doesn't want us to hear what the fortune teller has to say about her future?"

"Oh, for pity's sake." She balled up her napkin and got to her feet. "Let's get this over with."

She cast a longing glance at the gaming hall as they passed by, before being distracted by the festival. The street appeared much different in the daylight. Tents along both sides of the roadway zig-zagged down High Street to the train station below, looking like mushrooms that had popped up overnight. Costumed mimes stood frozen in place, breaking pose to mimic unsuspecting passersby, to the amusement of those watching.

In the daylight, she saw people of all ages here to enjoy the festival. The majority were well-dressed, the children wide-eyed as they clung to a parent's or sibling's hand.

"For the first time ever, the hotel is full," Maia announced. "Silver Springs Junction is finally being heralded as more than a train stop. Minerva and I spoke with a reporter fellow yesterday. He's writing about the festival for a newspaper in the East."

"I hope you told him to drop into the gambling hall while he's here."

"Yes, I told him to look for Beckett."

Selene clenched her teeth. No point in accusing Maia of undermining her. Her sister wouldn't have the faintest idea what she was talking about.

"Beckett said to watch for pickpockets," she said, tucking her reticule close as an unkempt man veered toward their little group. "Apparently an event like this attracts the unsavory sort as well as desirable."

After a long, speculative look at the four of them, the man veered in the opposite direction. In his stead, a group of acrobats on horseback rode down the middle of the street, delighting viewers as they stood on the backs of their mounts and successfully performed a series of moves that made Selene dizzy just watching.

The fortune teller's tent sat apart from the others, strung with colored flags flapping in the breeze, beckoning those wandering past to stop for a closer look.

Inside, an older woman was seated behind a crystal ball. She was adorned in dozens of scarves floating around her shoulders and bosom. Another was wrapped around her hair. Her beringed hands were shuffling a deck of cards in a way that told Selene she had done it countless times.

"Come in, ladies, come in," she said without looking up from the cards. "I've been expecting you."

Selene barely stifled a snort. Of course she had. Them or some other suckers. And surely it was a coincidence to see four chairs on the opposite side of the table from the woman, whose sign on the tent wall behind her read 'Madame Lazonga'.

She smiled at their group, revealing a gold tooth in front. Fortune telling must be lucrative.

"Sisters," she announced. "Riddled with questions. Don't be shy. Have a seat."

The others moved forward eagerly. Selene slid into the last chair.

Madame pushed her crystal ball to one side as she leaned forward, squinting as if to see them better. "I see sorrow and loss has accompanied you here today. If I possessed the power, I would summon your mama and your papa to join us and offer words of comfort, but that is not the gift I was blessed with."

"What is your gift?" Selene asked. "Besides separating unsuspecting victims from their money?"

"I was told to expect a cynic among you."

"Who told you that?"

The woman just smiled a secret smile as if privy to a joke the rest of them knew nothing about. "Who wants to be first to learn about her future?"

When no one spoke up, her smile widened. "Good idea. We'll let the cards decide."

She shuffled again, laid out an array of cards face down, then muttered a few unintelligible words before flipping over the card closest. It was like no ordinary playing card Selene had ever seen and she noticed the woman didn't ask any of them to cut the deck. Of course not. It was no doubt stacked the way she wanted it.

Madame Lazonga pursed her lips and squinted, then crooked a finger toward Chandra. "You. I see you with children. Not yours, though."

Big deal. How hard would it be to learn that Chandra sometimes took on the temporary care of hotel guests' children to give the parents a break. "I see a union. A young man. It happens fast. Almost before you are ready. And yet, it is the right choice for you, despite what others might think or say."

Chandra sent her sisters a smug look. "You're saying I'm more than capable of knowing my own mind."

Madame Lazonga laughed. "That is one trait shared among your sisters and you. There will be clashes. You will feel the loss. You may need to learn the art of compromise. But ultimately all will work out as the stars intended."

She flipped over a second card. This time her gaze found Minerva. "I see danger ahead. If not danger, deceit and misunderstandings. You must not believe everything others tell you, but decide for yourself what is right and what is wrong. This will take some time to accomplish, for there will be many false paths taken before you find the one meant for you."

"What does that mean?" Minerva asked.

The old woman waved her hand over the card, then clapped both hands together twice, setting her bracelets jangling.

"You have gifts. Learn to use them and you will eventually share them with others."

"I don't understand." Minerva looked as if she was about to burst into tears.

Selene couldn't believe her sister was taking any of this seriously.

"At this time you do not need to understand. But you will have help on your life course. In fact," she paused and leaned closer to the card. "I believe you may have already met one young man who will eventually alter your life course."

"Only one?" Selene asked sarcastically.

"There will definitely be more than one man who impacts your life." The other girls hooted with laughter at the idea of quiet, shy Minerva dealing with more than one suitor at a time.

Madame Lazonga flipped over a third card and pointed at Selene. "You. Impatient one."

That set her sisters off into a fresh spate of giggles.

"I am not impatient," Selene said.

Lazonga gave her a knowing look, one eyebrow arched. She exhaled heavily. "This plan you have. Be careful. It is destined to backfire."

Selene caught her breath. Not that she believed any of this hooey, but she couldn't bear it if the gambling hall turned out to be a flop. It couldn't! It wouldn't! She lifted her chin defiantly.

"I don't believe you."

"It doesn't matter. Whatever you think. For the die have already been cast."

Gambling talk. Lucky coincidence. Or again, word on the street about her affiliation with the hall.

Lazonga shrugged. Seeming unfazed by Selene's attitude, she moved on. One more card was flipped. This time Maia captured the fortune teller's full attention. "You. The patient one. As first born, you will be the last to marry."

The girls gasped. This was the first they'd heard about marriage. "You will meet soon, but the course will not be without its challenges. Take heart. He is worth the wait. He is your destiny."

Maia waited, poised on the edge of her seat as if she was hoping for more, but Lazonga gathered up her cards.

"A group reading is tiring. I must filter the energy brought inside by each of you."

"Of course. Thank you." Maia stood, fished some coins from her reticule and laid them on the table.

If it had been up to Selene, she wouldn't have given the woman a cent. On the other hand, everyone had the right to earn a living. Even a charlatan who took advantage of folks who were desperate, gullible or both. People sought her out of their own free will.

As they left, she listened with half an ear to the girls

chattering among themselves, wondering about Minerva's suitors and which fellow would be Maia's destiny.

"You'd best be careful," Chandra said to Selene. "Something you're up to is about to backfire on you."

"Which tells me, if this nonsense you dragged me along for is over and done with, I should get back to the gaming hall and circumvent anything untoward from happening." She also hadn't had the chance to speak to George about that noise in the walls that she and Lila had both heard. "Did you all know Lila is writing a mystery story? About a woman sleuth."

"Yes," Maia said. "She told us one day at tea when you weren't around."

"I wonder what Bolton thinks about it."

"He's pleased as punch that she's putting her talent to good use."

Selene doubted Bolton was as enthusiastic about his wife's pursuits as he pretended. The fact that he'd agreed to help Afi find them suitable husbands showed his true colors. Just another man who believed a woman's place was in the home.

Selene suffered being dragged through the rest of the festival before they finally turned around and headed back to the hotel.

Afi must have been waiting for their return. "There you are girls," he barked from the parlor. "Can you spare your poor old grandfather a few minutes of your time?"

"He's up to something," Selene hissed.

Maia gave her a superior look. "You're so suspicious. He probably just misses us. We've all been busier than usual, what with the hotel full and the town so crowded."

"Come in," Afi greeted them, smiling wider than usual. "Take a seat, won't you?"

Yup. Definitely the cat who swallowed the canary. Selene perched on the piano bench, while the others took positions on the chairs and settees artfully arranged around the room. Afi normally only used the room for entertaining, preferring his study or the dining room for family gatherings.

"It's quite something isn't it? Seeing our modest little town all tarted up and ready for our visitors."

"It's a real triumph," Maia said.

"A wonderful testament to your vision," Minerva added.

"We're all so proud of you," Chandra gushed.

Selene said nothing, quietly waiting. Not sure what she was waiting for. A visitor. An announcement. She could almost smell something afoot. Dare she hope the person responsible for the hotel thefts had been apprehended? Moments later she heard newcomers in the lobby. The distinct rise and fall of masculine voices.

Afi jumped to his feet and opened the door wide. "Bolton. Gentlemen. Please come in. Thank you for joining us."

Selene shot an 'I told you so' look at her sisters, as she rose and pasted on a smile. Her nightmare come to life. More than a dozen men, all shapes and sizes, hats in hand, milled around the parlor, introducing themselves. First to Afi, before turning their attention to Selene and her sisters. Just inside the door, looking mighty pleased with himself, stood Bolton.

CHAPTER 7

I f that wasn't the most mortifying situation she had ever been part of! Selene stood at the window and watched in disbelief as Bolton passed each man what appeared to be a folded bill or bills as they left. He'd paid them to show up! She didn't know if she should laugh at the ridiculousness of it or stomp her foot in disgust. If these same men showed up in the emporium at some point, she could only hope they didn't recognize her. Didn't view her as a pathetic spinster, whose grandfather went to such extreme lengths to see her married off.

She flung back her shoulders! All the more reason to get rid of Beckett. To have the emporium her triumph and hers alone. Step one of creating her own Holy Trinity. Success. Money. Power.

"CONGRATULATIONS!" Crawford joined Beckett, who stood well-back from the action of the newly-opened gambling hall. Some patrons circled the room, necks craned and eyes bugged as they stared at the chandeliers, the gaming tables, the oversize bar, the cashier cages. Others made a beeline to the tables. Beckett tried to hide his impatience. Crawford meant well, but he never had been able to stop himself from poking into projects long after he'd turned them over to others. There ought to be a name for that sort of meddling.

"You should be congratulating Selene." Beckett kept his eye on two men who had just entered the premises. Men he recognized from his earlier life.

"Selene's an intelligent girl and does a splendid job keeping the accounts for the hotel, but an undertaking of this caliber requires a man's capable hand."

"Selene is as capable as anyone."

"In many ways she's too capable," Crawford said. "But she's over her head here. The sooner she realizes that and steps away, the better."

Beckett shifted his attention from the newcomers who, after a quick scan of the main room, headed for one of the private game rooms. It was plain Crawford had something up his sleeve and it wasn't a Jack. "You knew from the outset I wouldn't stay here indefinitely."

"Of course."

"Besides which, I don't see Selene walking away."

"I'm trusting you to see that it happens. Subtly. Make it seem like her idea."

He narrowed his gaze. Yup, Crawford was up to something. "Getting embroiled with you and your family wasn't part of our arrangement. Or has it slipped your mind why I'm really here?"

"Not at all. We've both waited a long time to see Preston get his dues."

"And when he shows up, we'll be ready."

"We will be if Selene is safely out of the picture. She's

bound to lose interest in this place once she has a husband and family vying for her attention. Bolton's working on seeing quality men move here. Men with a firm enough hand for not only Selene, but all of my granddaughters."

"I hope I'm not included on that list of hopefuls. That Preston is the only reason for me being here."

Crawford laughed and clapped him on the shoulder. "We both know you're not the settling down type. No woman has ever held your interest longer than a day."

That wasn't necessarily true. Crawford knew a fair amount about his early days. But not everything. "I bet you had hopes for Bolton, though, didn't you? Shame he turned up with a bride in tow."

"I admit, Bolton's like the son I never had. Reminds me a lot of myself when I was younger. I would have gladly welcomed him into the family." He sighed. "Turned out I was too late."

Beckett's gaze was drawn across the room to Selene, trying to imagine her in the role of wife and mother. Tonight, she was breathtaking in a fetching gown of deep green, much like the one she'd worn for their night of cards. Her hair was intricately piled atop her head and adorned with several diamond pins that glittered in the light of the overhead chandeliers. Her smile was warm, greeting the folks who came through the door as if she was welcoming them into her home. Couldn't Crawford see that she belonged here?

Several well-dressed women were among the new arrivals, and staff members were on hand collecting coats and wraps in exchange for proffered glasses of champagne for the ladies. While the grand opening was clearly a success, the true measure would come later. Once the novelty wore off. After the festival was over and things in town returned to normal. That's when the real work began to ensure the gambling hall's ongoing success.

"Excuse me," he said to Crawford. "I need to check on a few things."

A few things being Selene, who was no longer by the door. He'd hoped her position there would keep her busy. No such luck. And when he found her in one of the private gaming rooms, pinned in a corner by Rogers and Kelley, his blood boiled. Trust those two to hone in on her, sensing her lack of experience. They were card sharks. Cheaters, but accomplished ones. Banned by the riverboats, he'd heard they'd headed West. No surprise they'd shown up here.

"Evening, gentlemen," he said stepping between them and Selene, placing a proprietorial hand on her arm. "Please excuse me if I spirit this lady away. Her presence is required elsewhere."

"That was rude," Selene said once they were out of earshot. "Those gentlemen were most intrigued by our operation."

"I'm sure they were," Beckett was grimly, releasing his hold. "They've been banned from most gambling establishments in several states."

"Oh." She clasped her elbows across her midriff, a move which thrust her bosom upward.

"They're very good at sniffing out an establishment's weakness and working it to their advantage. Whether it's an inexperienced dealer or a novice player they can manipulate."

"Are you saying we should ban them too?"

"Nope. They need to be watched, is all."

She tilted her head his way, her green eyes troubled. "If you know who they are, why didn't they recognize you?"

"I was always careful not to attract their notice. A few of my friends were not so lucky."

"You have friends?" Cynicism tinged her words.

He let the insult pass. Despite the fancy gown and hairdo, she was nervous. "A few besides Crawford."

"What do we do? About those two?"

"For now, nothing. I'll keep an eye on them."

She straightened and faced him head on. "I know exactly what you're doing, Beckett. You're trying to make a point. Show me I don't have the experience or the skills to manage things here on my own."

He blew out an impatient breath. She'd never believe he was doing the total opposite. Doing all he could to leave her in good stead, able to accomplish whatever she set her mind to.

"I know you assigned me door duty to keep me busy."

He bit back a smile. "You are a natural hostess. But I did wonder how long before you abandoned your post."

"And?"

He pulled out his timepiece. "You stuck it out longer than I expected."

He placed a hand on either side of her jaw and turned her head gently. "See that fellow at the bar? The one in the bowler hat?"

She nodded. "Near the end."

"That's Ryder Lyon. He's some sort of newspaper hack. I think now would be a good time to stroll over and have a word."

"My sisters mentioned him. Does 'hack' mean what I think?"

"A journalist for hire who writes what he's told to write, often to sway public opinion."

"Maybe I can win him over." She started off.

He grabbed her arm and pulled her back to his side. "I meant both of us."

"You don't think I can handle one two-bit writer on my own?"

"I'm not worried about you, Selene. I'm worried about him."

SELENE GLIDED across the room one step ahead of Beckett, aware she still had a lot to learn. When approached by those two men earlier she'd been unsure of herself, secretly relieved when Beckett appeared. The journalist was an entirely different matter.

"Mr. Lyon," Beckett said. "Welcome to Silver Springs Emporium." He signaled to the bartender to top up Lyon's glass. "Allow me to buy you a drink."

Selene cleared her throat noisily. Beckett's eyes crinkled with amusement as he took Selene's hand and drew her forward. "I wanted to make sure you had a chance to meet Miss Crawford."

"Pleasure." Lyon raised his glass in acknowledgement. "I've already had occasion to meet your lovely sisters at the hotel."

"So they mentioned," Selene said. "My associate, Mr. Thompson has been invaluable as we readied things for tonight's grand opening."

"Congratulations all around. Not only for hosting the first annual summer solstice festival, but creating a gaming hall worthy of a royal visit."

"It was a team effort," Selene said sweetly. "What brings you to our humble town?"

"Always on the lookout for a newsworthy story. Word has

it Silver Springs Junction is poised for much bigger things than being a railway town. That the hotel and gaming hall are just the beginning."

"You make it sound like an ambitious undertaking. We're really just simple settlers, aren't we Mr. Thompson?"

His eyes were laughing at her. "If you say so, Miss Crawford."

Lyon was looking from one to the other with undisguised interest. "I've got a nose for a story, and I definitely smell one here. When can we all sit down together?"

Selene looked at Beckett as if she were incapable of making such a monumental decision without consulting him.

"Why don't you be our guest at the hotel tomorrow morning for breakfast? That way you'll get to meet the entire family, including the legendary Benjamin Crawford himself."

"It would be an honor," Lyon said.

"Until then," Beckett said, with a proprietary hand on the small of her back. "Good luck at the tables."

"I never gamble," Lyon said.

"Never trust a man who claims not to gamble," Beckett said, once they were out of earshot. "Life is a gamble. Coming West is a gamble. Anyone who thinks different is a fool."

"I find it equally difficult to trust a man who made his mark as a professional gambler."

"These days I've refined my risks. Moved away from places like this that are designed to take your money." His hand remained against the small of her back as he guided her across the hall, weaving between the tables and players.

Hmmm. If he no longer gambled for money, what did he consider worth gambling for? A shiver ran from the base of her skull and down her neck to land between her shoulder blades. Wouldn't it be something if it was her? And for once in his life, Beckett Thompson lost.

DESPITE BECKETT'S insistence that he could handle closing the emporium on his own, Selene stayed till the end. The first sign of weakness and he'd think he had her. That Afi was right, the place was too much for her. Finally, the door closed on the last of the stragglers; the winners jubilant, the losers morose, the staff tired. Rather than be fatigued by the lateness of the hour, Selene felt more awake and alive than ever. As she locked the safe, hidden behind a sliding panel in the office, triumph coursed through her veins. She had done it!

Flushed with success and not watching her surroundings, she straightened, turned abruptly, and collided with Beckett. As she struggled for balance, he steadied her, his hands on her waist. The air in the room crackled, like warning of an approaching storm. A warning Selene should have heeded. Instead, she locked gazes with him. An unspoken challenge passed between them, seconds before he lowered his head and his lips found hers.

Beckett hadn't been the first man she'd kissed. There had been several young men over the years, anxious to try their luck with one of the Crawford heiresses. They all bored her. Even their kisses bored her. She'd never seen any big deal about this particular act of intimacy. Until Beckett!

Last time had been a whim. One which could have turned into more, but didn't. Tonight felt different. Touch overrode all other senses, made breathing difficult and coherent thought impossible. As his mouth plundered hers, desire spilled through her, saturating her limbs. Her legs took on the consistency of melted wax. Followed by a needful throbbing in her nether regions. Her bosom, squashed against his chest, tingled and nearly spilled from the top of her gown.

She longed to peel away her bodice. To feel the firmness of his palms on her—

She clasped her hands in his. Inched them slowly upward from her waist to her ribs. What if she...allowed certain liberties? If he were to become enamored, she could use it to her advantage. Make him her ally. Have him intervene on her behalf with her grandfather.

Sanity returned. She ripped her lips from beneath his and stepped back, as out of breath as if she'd run up the mountain and back. She didn't need a man to be her champion.

He watched her from beneath hooded lids, as if waiting to see her next move.

She threw back her head and laughed. She was too shaken to do anything else. It wasn't like her to let her emotions override common sense. While kissing Beckett, she'd nearly lost sight of her ambitions. Of succeeding on her own.

Admittedly, she enjoyed his kiss. And was curious to see what happened next. But she couldn't allow it. Such a move would make her seem weak. Surrendering control. At least, Beckett was sure to see it that way.

"Is that your latest gamble?" she asked. "Kiss me and see where things lead?"

His face remained inscrutable. "We both know where things could lead. Question is, is it the right thing to do?"

Her body might scream 'yes'. Yes, please! Her mind knew it was not. Selene pressed her lips together to stop them from tingling. To stop herself from wanting him. The settee in the corner of the office beckoned. Too tempting. Far too convenient.

"No more than it was right of my grandfather to undermine my work here."

"I agree. In fact, I've told him as much. That you are more than capable of making a success of the emporium. Unfortunately, he's old-fashioned."

"You agree? Does that mean you'll leave me to do things as I see fit?"

"There's something I need to see to first. Details of which I can't disclose. Do you trust me?"

He stared down at her, waiting for her answer.

"Why should I?"

His mouth tightened, his eyes mirroring his disappointment. Was it because she didn't acquiesce to their desires? Or because she did not fully trust him? "That's not the answer I was hoping for."

Not for either of them.

Closing and locking the office behind them, she straightened to face him. "I know what you're doing, Beckett. You think you can appease us both. Manage me in a way that satisfies both you and Afi."

His eyes raked her from top to toe. "I doubt Crawford and I have the same needs to be satisfied."

She pretended to misunderstand. "Right now, your needs coincide with mine. The success of this venture. And hosting Mr. Lyon for breakfast tomorrow. I'm certain he can be most useful."

As they reached the main hall, Beckett extinguished the lights. Moonlight from the full moon spilled through the window and illuminated a path to the door, bathing everything in its silvery hue. Selene hoped it was a good omen.

As they crossed the street to the hotel, faint sounds from the festival could be heard in the distance. A slight breeze carried the occasional whiff of bonfire smoke. "It's only Day One of the festival. Afi's future plans include a month-long event, attracting performers and patrons from as far away as Europe."

"Crawford's larger-than-life ambitions have, in part, led to his success."

Selene nodded, pushing aside a niggle of worry. Beckett was right. Right now, Afi's driving ambition was to see her and her sisters wed. He was unlikely to rest until he got his way.

"Good night," she said, once they reached the hotel. "Thank you for your—guidance this evening."

"Pleasant dreams," Beckett said. "You'll need to be at your best in the morning for our guest."

"I'm always at my best."

CHAPTER 8

Despite her late evening Selene rose early, only to enter the breakfast room and find others already there. Beckett was seated next to Afi, with Bolton on her grandfather's other side. The three men were speaking among themselves, their voices too low for her to catch what was being said.

She stood in the doorway, arms crossed over her chest, and cleared her throat noisily. They all looked up. Was that guilt? Had she been the topic of conversation?

"Good morning, gentlemen. Don't let me interrupt," she said as she strolled to the sideboard and poured herself a cup of tea from the silver service.

Afi made a noise as if something was strangling him. "Beckett was just filling us in on the writer fellow. We were discussing how much information about the town and the hotel and our future plans we wanted to share."

"Should I not be included in that conversation?" She took a seat and reached for a slice of toast from the holder, pulling the crystal serving dish of marmalade toward her.

Afi didn't respond to her question. "Beckett tells me you

two are getting along royally in your endeavors across the street."

Especially if you counted last night's kiss.

"We have the same goals," she said, sending Beckett a satisfied smile. "Isn't that right?"

Before he could comment, the desk clerk appeared in the doorway with Ryder Lyon behind him. 'This gentleman says he's expected?"

"Quite right." Beckett beat Selene to his feet. "We're glad you could make it."

Selene stepped forward to make the introductions between Lyon, her grandfather and Bolton. Beckett's gaze clashed with hers across the table as Afi proceeded to grill the newcomer about his credentials, asking who he had worked for in the past, what sort of reporting he did, factual or sensational, and who made up his audience. Selene missed his response but whatever he said earned a gruff laugh of approval from her grandfather. Ryder must have passed the test, for Afi waved an expansive hand toward the sideboard, encouraging Ryder and the others to fill their plates.

Selene joined the men, torn between scrambled eggs or French toast, and ham or bacon. Minerva arrived just as she sat down. Her sister started into the room, then froze when she caught sight of Ryder.

Selene rose in alarm. She'd never seen Minerva so flushed. "Do you have a fever?"

Minerva gave her head a little shake. "I am quite well, thank you. I wasn't aware we were expecting guests."

Ryder swung around at the sound of her voice. "Miss Crawford. What an unexpected pleasure to have you join us."

Crawford spared a speculative frown. "I take it you two have met?"

"We have," Ryder said.

The room fell silent, save the rhythmic tick of the clock on the far wall.

Crawford cleared his throat. "Mr. Lyon has ties with several newspapers out East. He thinks a story about our little town might be of interest to Eastern folk. Too late for this year, but if I have my way next year's festival will be bigger and better."

"I have no doubt," Minerva said. "If you'll excuse me, I just remembered something I need to see to."

"But you haven't eaten a thing," Crawford said.

"I'm not really hungry." Minerva turned and rushed from the room.

"Selene," Crawford said. "Any idea what that's about?"

"Not in the least," Selene said. She hadn't set any store in what the fortune teller told them yesterday, but what if Minerva had? She frowned. What had Madame Lazonga said? Something about a young man altering the course of Minerva's life. Surely, Minerva wasn't pinning her hopes on the reporter? No, her sister was too sensible for that.

As the conversation resumed, Selene sipped her second cup of tea and listened to the others. Bolton was uncharacteristically silent. Lyon was complimentary when speaking of the town and the emporium, which seemed to be Afi's cue to wax elegant regarding his visions for the town.

"Chose this spot not only for its natural beauty, but so many individual rail lines converging makes it an easy destination to reach from every part of the country."

"A destination town," Lyon said. "One that doesn't rely on industry or natural resources. It's an interesting concept."

"This area has seen enough mining operations go bust,"

Afi said. "It needs a solid anchor. Folks hereabouts need to work, to build a stake in the area, and not everyone is cut out to be a farmer or a rancher."

Lyon nodded, scribbling in a notebook he'd pulled from his inside jacket pocket.

Selene hadn't thought about the town in those terms. Listening to Afi, her admiration grew. The hotel and gambling hall were a draw, and offered year-round work for people in the area. But as her grandfather spoke, expressive hand gestures punctuating his words, she could see his vision coming to life. Silver Springs Junction, a busy, vibrant town with shops, schools, a church, cafes and financial institutions. A place people moved to and put down roots. Perhaps even a hospital one day. And art. They needed scholars. Artists and writers. The town could sponsor a contest. Encourage artists to compete, then choose a winner to erect an artistic focal point for the town square. By the time Afi wound down she was so worked up she could barely sit still. All her dreams seemed suddenly within reach.

A moment later reality intruded with a rude thud. She couldn't possibly be the driving force behind the growth and activity she foresaw. The emporium was more than enough to keep her busy. Unless—

She looked over at Beckett.

No! She was not turning the gambling hall over to him so she was free to chase a whimsy. The Silver Springs Junction Afi spoke of was years from becoming a reality. Better to be content with what she had; what she'd created.

"I hope you'll let your readers know the sort of high-end gaming establishment they'll find here when they visit Silver Springs Junction."

Why was the room so suddenly silent? People shifted in

their seats avoiding eye contact with the others in the room. Why did she get the sense something was going on here that she knew nothing about? Could it have been the conversation she'd interrupted when she arrived?

"You can count on that, Miss Crawford." Lyon tucked away his notebook, thanked everyone for breakfast, then took his leave.

"You're quiet, Bolton," Selene said. She was still smarting after seeing him pay off those men he'd paraded through as prospective husbands. Men ought to be paying for a chance to meet a Crawford heiress. Not the other way.

"Just thinking," Bolton said. "Does anyone know exactly how long Mr. Lyon has been in town?"

"Why?"

"I've been told this is not his first visit. Although his story for being here provides a ready cover."

"A cover for what?" Selene was confused.

"It gives him the perfect excuse to be nosing around. Especially if he's our thief."

Bolton was pretending to be carrying on with that charade, was he? Pretending he wasn't really here to find them all husbands, but was on the hunt for a thief. Selene sniffed loudly. She knew better.

When no one responded, Selene rose. The men did as well. She waited. No one moved. So this is what it came down to. They were waiting for her to leave so they could return to the secret discussion they'd been having before she arrived. Her gaze moved belligerently from one to the next, daring them to take their leave. No one met her eyes except Beckett, who appeared amused. She let out a deep sigh. No point hanging around where she clearly was not wanted.

"I'll go check on Minerva."

She found her sister in the art room, staring at a blank sheet of paper on the easel.

"Waiting for inspiration to strike?"

Minerva whirled, looking as guilty as if Selene had caught her with the proverbial hand in the cookie jar.

"Where are the others?" Selene asked, puzzling over Minerva's actions. Less than a year apart in age, their younger selves had a connection similar to that shared by some twins, who were privy to each other's moods and secret thoughts. The gift had gradually paled as they entered adulthood. Selene missed those days. At least, she missed knowing what was going on in Minerva's head. It was best that Minerva, the most sensitive of the sisters, not know what was going on with her.

"They're at the festival."

"Let's go look for them."

With a last, resigned look toward the blank easel, Minerva nodded.

"IT DOESN'T APPEAR the party shut down last night," Selene said as several bleary-eyed men stumbled past them in rumpled clothing, a sour smell permeating the air. Bonfires smoldered, their charred remains a reminder of last evening's festivities.

Minerva raised a delicate, lace-edge hankie to her nose. "Apparently not."

"A full moon at solstice. Beckett said it's quite the rare occurrence."

"You've been spending a lot of time with him lately," Minerva said.

"It's not like I was given a choice." Underlying bitterness tinged her words.

"I do wish Afi would stop treating us like youngsters that he's humoring," Minerva said vehemently.

"I didn't know you felt that way."

"Last year I wanted to go to Paris to study art. He told me it's rife with drunks and bohemians, no place for a well-bred young lady."

She nodded. Unlikely Afi would let Minerva, or any of them, out from under his watchful eye.

"It would be different were I a man. No one is stopping that reporter fellow from traveling around the country. No one would stop him if he took it into his head to go to Paris."

"Don't forget, Afi took us all over with him when we were young. I expect we've seen far more of the country than most people."

"Until he planted us here."

Selene laughed. "Where we're expected to propagate and make him a great-grandfather."

Minerva sniffed. "I need to be around other artists. People with a creative mindset."

"I wonder—" Selene said.

"Wonder what?"

Lots of things. Particularly what the men were avidly discussing when she wasn't in the room. She forced her thoughts to Minerva.

"Afi said he intends to make the festival bigger and better next year. There must be a way to encourage the involvement of artists as well as entertainers."

"Oh, Selene. I love you! What a totally brilliant idea!"

"Is it? Oh, good. Let me know what I can do to help."

"Help?" It was amusing to watch Minerva flounder. "But it's your idea."

"Which I, in turn, am gifting to you, sister dearest. I have more than enough projects of my own to chase."

Minerva dug in her feet, lips thinned, eyes flashing a challenge. "Remember *Little Women*? We need to stick together like the March sisters."

Selene raised a brow. "Supporting each other does not mean we live each other's dreams. We each need to follow our own destiny. And support each other even though our choices might be different." She bit off her words. Where had that thought even come from? She gazed skyward. Sometimes it felt as if dear, departed mama was looking down on her, guiding her thoughts. Letting her know when she disapproved certain actions.

Minerva sighed in reluctant agreement. "Someone needs to explain to Afi that the four of us are not all cut from the same cloth. Surely you don't plan to spend all your time at the gambling hall?"

"I do if I want to protect my interests. Otherwise Beckett will take over completely." And never leave the town. She only partly believed him when he'd said something else had brought him here. Something he wasn't at liberty to discuss with her. Which reminded her. She needed to start work on 'project Beckett'. Find him a love interest.

For now, she'd pretend to be enamored with his company, at least in front of Afi. That way she could act as shocked and disappointed as anyone when Beckett fell for someone else and moved away. Pretending to suffer a broken heart would also give her a reprieve from any other matchmaking efforts from Afi or Bolton. She smiled to herself and linked her arm through Minerva's. She liked this plan.

"Oh, look." Minerva pointed. "A magician's tent. It looks like he's just starting his act."

Selene shook her head. She did not see the fascination with the festival performers. As far as she was concerned the acts were all smoke and mirrors. Like the self-proclaimed fortune teller, Madama Lazonga. Reluctantly she followed her sister inside where they were soon joined by Chandra. Their youngest sister seemed equally fascinated as the magician separated supposedly inseparable hoops, pulled a coin from behind a youngster's ear, then dazzled the crowd with a number of card tricks and other sleight of hand moves. As the performance drew to a close, Selene had seen enough and happily left her sisters to wait for the second show. At least Minerva seemed to be over her earlier melancholy.

Inside the hotel lobby, a lone woman on the far settee looked up from the book on her lap, closed the book abruptly and tucked it out of sight. Selene was immediately intrigued. Was the woman concerned someone might question her choice of reading material?

"Good morning," Selene said. "I didn't mean to startle you."

The woman's hands fluttered like a baby bird who had fallen from its nest. A faint pink stained her cheeks, as if she was unaccustomed to being the object of attention. She was plain but not homely, near Selene's age.

"That's all right. I—I didn't think anyone would mind if I sat here quietly."

"I'm sure no one does." Selene paused. "Are you in town for the festival?"

"Oh, no." The other woman shook her head vehemently.

"Bad timing then," Selene said. "Normally it's rather quiet here. I'm Selene Crawford, by the way. My grandfather owns this hotel."

The other woman's eyes grew round as saucers. "You live here?"

"Afraid so," Selene said with a lift of her brows. "And you are—?"

The woman cast her gaze to her lap. "Deirdre Mathers. I'm here with my father, Pastor Mathers."

A pastor's daughter? She liked the sound of that.

Without being invited, Selene perched on the opposite end of the settee. "What brings you and your father to these parts?"

"The Lord's work," Deirdre said. "Always." Her words were punctuated with a sigh.

"Just the two of you?"

Deirdre nodded as she stared down at her hands clasped in her lap. That single gesture gave Selene a glimpse into the other woman's life, moving about the country with a man more intent on tending a new flock than his own child. What if she hadn't had her sisters for companionship as Afi moved them from place to place, never staying anywhere long enough to make friends, schooled by a revolving door of tutors and governesses?

And wouldn't a pastor's daughter be a perfect match for Beckett? Someone used to doing as she was told. Someone in need of his protection.

"That must be lonely," Selene said. "I grew up with three sisters, which meant things were never dull."

Deirdre's look grew wistful. "When I was younger, I prayed for a sister."

"Tell you what." Selene rose. "Be our guest this evening for supper. I'll introduce you to mine." And to Beckett, if she could possibly arrange it.

As if she'd conjured him from thin air, Beckett descended the stairs to the lobby. "Beckett!" As Selene waved him over, she saw a brief flash of surprise before he masked his expression and strode across the lobby toward them.

"I wanted to introduce you to Miss Mathers. I've just invited her to join us for the evening meal. It would be lovely if you could join us as well."

Beckett's eyes narrowed as his gaze roved from her to Deirdre and back to her. "I'm afraid I have plans this evening. Miss Mathers, welcome to Silver Springs Junction."

Deirdre rose and bobbed in a slight curtsy as if she were greeting royalty. Selene ground her teeth. Now she'd be stuck with the woman, while Beckett was no doubt doing something far more interesting.

Beckett's gaze found Selene. "It seems prudent at least one of us be at the emporium during the evening hours."

"Right you are." She turned to Miss Mathers. "Perhaps I can interest you in a tour of the emporium after our meal."

"Father claims games of chance are the work of the devil," Deirdre said demurely.

Beckett quirked one brow at Selene. "Right, then. I'll see you later."

After he left, Selene turned to Deirdre with false animation. "Your father would appreciate knowing Beckett is a reformed man, and no longer pursues games of chance."

"Father is big on forgiveness," Deirdre said. "But I fear he would look askance at anyone who enables others in their vice."

"Tell me. What brought you and your father to Silver Springs Junction?"

"Father heard about the gambling institution and felt it was his calling to help steer folks from evil. The pagan festival further convinced him that folks here are in desperate need of the word of the Lord."

"I see."

"I fear, as kind as it was of you to invite me, he would disapprove of my dining with you and your sisters."

"I understand," Selene said. Clearly Deirdre was not the one to lure Beckett far from Silver Springs Junction. However, she wasn't about to abandon her scheme just because of one minor setback.

SELENE UNLOCKED the door to the gambling emporium. No one was expected for at least an hour when staff from the hotel would descend to spit and polish every inch of the place under the eagle eye of Miriam, the hotel's head housekeeper. Unlike other gambling institutions, the emporium did not remain open day and night, which helped maintain exclusivity. That and the dress code. Unkempt, unshaven rowdies seeking a game of chance were not welcome here.

Thick carpet muffled her steps as she moved from room to room, trying to pinpoint the reason for this nagging sense of discontent plaguing her ever since she rose. Yesterday she had been flushed with triumph. Today her victory felt hollow.

She trailed her fingers over the gleaming wood of a roulette table. Word of the emporium's triumphant opening night would spread through the territory like wild fire, helped along by reporters such as Ryder Lyon. Afi's golden horseshoes were firmly in place, meaning Silver Springs Junction and its hotel were a guaranteed success. Along with the emporium and the festival.

But was it truly *her* success?

Why did it feel like something was missing?

In the office, she checked the sliding panel that secreted the safe.

"All secure?"

She whirled. Beckett stood in the doorway behind her. As the carpet had muffled her steps, it had also muffled his.

"Why wouldn't it be?"

"I was on my way here when I was stopped by several of last night's patrons."

Naturally they would approach Beckett! Despite changes across the country, suffrage and women securing the vote in some states, it remained very much a man's world.

"It seems several of our guests last evening returned home minus personal items of value."

"A thief?" Selene swallowed a growing sense of dread. First in the hotel, and now here. This was very bad news.

"Yes. Odd anyone would target folks here rather than the festival goers."

Selene thought about the rough-looking man who'd been eyeing her reticule in the street the other day. Someone dressed like that would have been escorted out straight away, if they even made it through the door to begin with.

"It had to be a well-dressed thief or thieves," she said. "Men or women who blended in easily."

"There's also the chance that picking pockets wasn't their primary target, but an irresistible side endeavor."

"I don't understand."

Beckett looked grim. "We're dealing with a sophisticated, well-organized group of thieves after far bigger fish. A few members could have been sent ahead to case the place, and were unable to resist a few easy marks while they were at it. Or their actions were a deliberate attempt to throw us off their main objective."

Selene's shoulders sagged. Getting Beckett out of her hair was a minor issue compared to thwarting a would-be gang of thieves.

"What about those two men you recognized? The ones you said had been banned from other gambling establishments?"

"They're card sharks, not thieves. The thrill for them is cheating without getting caught."

"Don't all men feel that way?" She raised a brow. "Not only in games of chance."

Beckett cocked his head. "Gleaned from personal experience?"

"You could say." Ever since her figure filled out, she'd seen the hungry looks sent her way by men, wives at their sides. It was only one of the reasons she'd vowed to never marry. In many states, wives were still considered the property of their husbands.

"From now on, no one is to be here alone. Not you. Not I. No one on staff, early or late." Before she could protest, he added. "I recall you own a pistol."

Their eyes met. Unlikely she'd forget that night in the darkened hotel when a noise had sent them both on the prowl. Her pistol had ended up against his midsection. She nodded. "Afi saw to us having a very well-rounded education."

"Get in the habit of having it on you at all times."

She swallowed her resentment at the way he took charge. There were more important things to worry about. "All right." She'd need to brush up on her marksmanship and make sure her sisters did the same. "Anything else?"

"I suggest we make our primary safe a decoy. Stash a small amount of cash and some random papers in there. Nothing important."

"And where do you suggest we keep the bulk of cash?"

"I have a few ideas."

She eyed him closely. Afi trusted the man. But what if Beckett had changed? No longer a professional gambler, what if he was a con man, doing and saying all this to throw her off?

How dreadful not knowing who, if anyone, she could trust.

"I'm not the threat here, Selene."

She lifted her chin to meet his gaze. He thought he knew her so well. She sidled closer. "Are you sure?"

Then she rose up on tiptoe and pressed her lips to his.

CHAPTER 9

Beckett slid one hand around Selene's waist, pinning her against him while he tumbled his other hand through her hair, sending pins flying. She was the most contradictory minx. As changeable as the weather, hot one moment, cool the next. She had an astute head for business, unerring skills for dealing with people, and a body that fit against his far too well.

What man could resist the inviting warmth of her mouth? The lush cushion of her bosom cradling his chest. He heard her moan softly in the back of her throat as he deepened the kiss before he trailed his fingertips from her luxurious hair down the side of her neck, feeling her pulse jump and her breath catch. Her tongue teased his and she raised her hands to clasp his jaw, anchoring him in place.

Heat coursed through his blood as he slid his hands around her ribs to march them up and down her back. She pressed herself tighter against him in exquisite torture before he reluctantly ended the kiss. Her eyes remained on his, her head cocked to one side. He smiled down at her with his best poker face.

He knew exactly what she was up to. Attempting to disarm and distract him. A part of him wondered how far she'd take things. It might be interesting to find out, but the price was too great. Gambling his future to get tangled up with Selene was a risk he wasn't willing to take.

He needed to keep his focus sharp. Be prepared for the opportunity to beat an old enemy at his own game. He and Crawford believed Silver Springs Junction, along with the Gambling Emporium, would prove a temptation that swine Preston couldn't resist.

He stepped back, his gaze sweeping the room. "Where would you consider the most secure place to stash the day's take before we move it to the vault over at the hotel?"

Their initial plan involved shifting the money from the office safe once or twice a week at random times and different days of the week. "I should ask Afi when he plans to finish the tunnel."

"Tunnel?"

She nodded. "Another of Afi's eccentricities. We were of age before he told us about the tunnel beneath the hotel. I guess he didn't want us getting trapped down there when we were little. Earlier last year, when the emporium was being constructed, he opted to have a branch lead over here. He used a crew of ex-miners who aren't from the area to construct it."

Cagey old bugger. "So the men who worked on this place don't know there was a tunnel from the hotel?" Wasn't that interesting!

She shook her head and moved toward the bar. He joined her, resisting the temptation to rest his hands atop her shoulders, to pull her back against him and bury his mouth against the enticing soft curve where shoulder met neck. He already knew her taste and scent were intoxicating. And like any addiction, best to be avoided.

At that second, she met his gaze in the mirror. Her mouth curved in a secret smile, as if she knew the inner torment she was putting him through.

"How about this?" She rapped her knuckles on the top of the massive wooden bar crafted from half a giant tree, flat on top with a curving underbelly.

"What about it." He stroked the bar top which almost felt as if it was still alive.

"After it had been felled, loggers discovered the tree's center was rotten. Since I had my heart set on it, I had the wood carver hollow out the core and attach the top in a way that the structure looks like solid wood."

"The top alone must weight hundreds of pounds. It's not something you or I could lift off and on."

"Actually, you're wrong. The master craftsman who created it came up with the brilliant idea of using piano hinges. I thought the inside might be useful for storage at some point. I never thought about a cache for money."

"Show me."

Selene rounded the bar, moved a tray of glasses onto the shelf behind her, and placed the heel of her hand under the lip in such a way that the top lifted noiselessly and stayed there without her holding it in place. The deep cubby hole was large enough to hide a full-grown man.

He stepped back and studied the rounded belly of the bar, rough in areas with patches of bark. He never would have guessed. "It looks like a solid half tree."

"That's the idea." She closed the top as easily as she had opened it and spun to face him. "What do you think?"

"All we need is the right size safe. Secured in a way it

can't be removed." It just happened he knew exactly where to get one. "Does anyone else know the bar top moves?"

She caught her lower lip with her teeth, which meant she was thinking. "The bar was brought in all of a piece. It's possible the men moving it noticed it wasn't as heavy as they were expecting, but no one mentioned it."

Beckett slapped it with the palm of his hand. "I'll look after getting a second safe."

"And in the meantime?"

"In the meantime, I want to see this tunnel."

A MYRIAD OF questions ran through Selene's mind as she and Beckett reached the hotel. It had been bad enough learning jewelry thefts were happening here. At least they'd been able to take precautions. But at the gambling hall? Taking advantage of guests whose attention was focused elsewhere? She could hardly insist their patrons check all valuables at the door with their coats. Worse yet. What if Beckett was right and last night was the precursor to a larger-scale theft?

Would thieves be so bold as to mount a stick-up at gunpoint when the emporium was open? Or wait until no one was there and attempt to crack the safe? Now she knew why Afi's hair was snow-white. He'd always said it was from raising her and her sisters. More likely it was a result of being constantly on guard against unscrupulous parties trying to get their hands on the wealth of others.

They were crossing the lobby when she got a frantic hand signal from Maia, who was at the front desk speaking to a smartly-dressed, middle-aged couple. The man was waving his arms through the air in jerky, agitated motions.

The woman stood with her arms folded across her midsection, her mouth set in a straight line.

"We'd better see what all this is about," she said, tugging Beckett by the sleeve of his jacket toward the trio.

"Good morning, Maia," she said, including the older couple in her smile. "Anything we can do to help?"

"Are you the law?" the man barked at Beckett.

"Just a concerned guest of the hotel," Beckett said smoothly. "Is there a problem?"

"I'll say there's a problem. We were robbed last night. Someone came in our room while we slept and helped themselves to the missus's jewel case. Everything's gone, case and all. And now this, this woman informs me there is no local sheriff. The closest lawman is in the next town over. Meanwhile the streets are crawling with thieves and ruffians, and no one here to do a thing about it."

"I gather you chose not to avail yourselves of the hotel's safe to store your valuables," Selene said.

"We didn't see the need," said the man.

"I never know until the last minute which piece I'd like to wear," the woman added.

"That's perfectly understandable," Beckett said. Selene slid her gaze his way. It pained her to admit it, but it was helpful to have another man present. Already the husband appeared calmer, his arms no longer thrashing about.

"We came to check out the town," he said. "I'm looking to expand my haberdashery business west and one of our sons told us about Silver Springs Junction. We didn't know about the festival."

"If you're looking for new business opportunities, you've certainly come to the right place. I'd be happy to arrange with the owner of the hotel for someone to show you around. You're very smart to set your sights on an up and coming place like this one to expand your operation. Would your son be the one running the western division?"

"We haven't gotten that far yet." The man preened at the compliment. "But I would like to get the lay of the land before I take things any further."

"While we wait for the sheriff to arrive, my sister and her staff will conduct their own investigation. If your jewels are in this town, I guarantee we'll find them," Selene said.

The woman looked at her husband, who nodded. "Most of those gemstones were paste anyway. The originals are safely locked away in a bank back home."

"The thieves won't know that. In the meantime, you can sleep soundly knowing there won't be a repeat," Maia said. "We'll have round the clock security keeping an eye out."

Beckett looked at Maia. "Do you think Mr. Crawford might be available to confer with Mr. and Mrs.—?" He paused and looked at the guests.

"Knightly," the man said. "I've heard of Crawford. Do you really think he'd have time to see us?"

Maia stepped forward, obviously relieved. "I'm certain of it. If you don't mind coming with me?"

As the trio left, Selene turned to Beckett. "Thank you for defusing what could have been an ugly situation if other guests had overheard those two. Do you think it's the same ones who robbed our patrons last night?"

"Different MO," Beckett said. "Pickpockets tend to hit one area hard, then move on before their victims grow wise to them. Now, how do we access this tunnel?"

It sounded as if thieves and gamblers had a lot in common. Selene led the way to the hall behind the grand staircase. "Do you ever get tired of always being on the move?" When she was young Afi had moved them so often that it had been a relief to settle here. To finally call a place home.

"Nope. I get bored if I'm in one place for too long."

Her ears perked up. Happy news. As soon as the emporium was established, he'd grow bored and be on his way.

With a quick look over her shoulder to make sure no one was watching, she located the mechanism that slid the false panel aside. Beckett followed her inside and the panel slid closed behind them. She fumbled along the wall until she found a switch. Dim light illuminated a narrow staircase which disappeared into a black hole below.

"There should be a lantern at the bottom." The steps swayed slightly as she descended. Her feet hit solid ground and she found the lantern on a nail, next to a packet of Lucifer matches wedged in a cubby hole. She struck one and touched it to the wick. Beckett stared around in amazement at the opening to a tunnel nearly as tall as he was, shored in places with wooden supports.

She turned to him. "Satisfied?"

He placed one large hand on a wooden brace as if paying homage to the engineering. "Building this had to be quite the feat."

"I wouldn't know about that any more than I know why Afi kept it a secret. No one comes down here."

"I'm sure he had his reasons. Have you been in the branch that leads to the emporium?"

Selene bit her lip. Now was not the time to admit to a mild case of claustrophobia. "Stay down here if you like. I've got better things to do."

She blew out the lantern and replaced it on the nail before she grasped the railing and started up the steps, her heart racing faster than normal. The steps were definitely swaying beneath her weight. Another good reason to stay above ground.

It took forever to reach the top. She hoped Beckett didn't notice the way her hand shook slightly as she found the mechanism that slid the panel to one side. It wouldn't do for him to learn her phobia when it came to dark, enclosed spaces.

Beckett had barely stepped into the hall behind her when Bolton appeared. He frowned. "What are you two doing down there?"

"Beckett wanted to see what it was like."

"Crawford wants to see you. Both of you."

"Do you know if he met with the Knightlys?"

"Yes. He's arranged to give them a tour after tea."

Afi did not look pleased when they arrived in his study. "Bolton, you stay too," he barked.

As Selene stood before her grandfather, she felt like she was back in braids and short skirts, ten years old and about to be chastised for some mischief or other. Usually something Chandra concocted and bullied the others into going along with. Chandra never got blamed, even though she was behind most of their scrapes.

"I heard from several unhappy patrons who were robbed at the gaming hall last night. Then I have hotel guests telling me the same thing happened here. We need to put an end to this once and for all."

Selene and Beckett exchanged a look. Beckett gave her a barely perceptible nod to indicate she should speak first. Instead of the men speaking among themselves as if she wasn't there.

"Beckett and I are aware of what happened last night. He has a theory," Selene said.

"Let the man speak for himself," Afi snapped.

"I'm not finished," Selene snapped back.

Afi raised a brow but closed his mouth and sat back in his chair. "Very well. You have the floor."

When Beckett gave her an encouraging nod, Afi's eyes narrowed. "Dare I think you two are continuing to cooperate with each other?"

Selene bit back a smile. Afi was as changeable as the weather. "Isn't that what you had in mind when you stuck us together? At any rate, I think Beckett could be onto something. What if the jewelry thefts, at least those in the emporium, were intended to distract us from the thief's true intentions? To case out the place. Get a read on our nightly routines, the amount of cash we take in, where we store it and what type of security we have."

Afi looked at Beckett. "Could it be Preston?"

"What's a Preston?" Selene asked. It was happening again. Man-talk that excluded her.

"An old nemesis of Crawford and myself." Beckett turned and addressed her grandfather. "To answer your question, I haven't seen any evidence that he's involved, but he could have sent in a frontman to distract us."

"I have men watching all the train stations, set to alert me if it looks like he's headed this way," Afi said.

"No offense," Bolton spoke for the first time since they had assembled. "But it would be easy for Preston to don a disguise and pretend to be part of the festival."

Selene turned to Bolton. "I suppose everyone here is privy to the story of this mysterious Preston except me."

"I'll fill you in later," Beckett said. He turned to Afi. "For now, rest assured Selene and I have a plan."

Afi nodded. "I knew I was right to bring you in on the gaming hall."

Inwardly gritting her teeth, Selene smiled and batted her eyes. "You certainly were."

~

BECKETT COULD FEEL the sparks of irritation erupting from Selene as he ushered her back to the emporium where they could speak in private. Once inside she faced him, crossed her arms over her chest and waited.

He drew a breath. He shouldn't feel like he was going into battle, yet every day with Selene felt that way. "Crawford didn't bring me here because he thought you weren't capable of handling the place on your own. He just let you and everyone else think that."

"Why would he do that?"

"He felt, and I agreed, that the less people who knew why I was really here, the better."

Her eyes narrowed. "Who are you, really?"

He exhaled sharply before he spoke. When he did, his voice carried the drawl of the deep South. "Just a simple Southern boy whose family lost everything in the War. I had no skills beyond being trained to run our plantation. When the war ended, I scrambled to support my family to the best of my abilities. Eventually I met Crawford." He left out the part about never quite blocking out his father's voice. His old man had been broken by the war, but remained mean enough to try and bring down everyone around him. He never tired of telling Beckett he was nothing. Worthless.

Selene's eyes narrowed. "I never know what to believe coming out of your mouth. Up until now you sounded as Northern as anyone I've ever met."

He smirked. "Dialect is one of my talents."

"What does that have to do with this nemesis of yours and Afi's?"

"Nothing. Years ago, Preston headed up one of the largest merchant banks in the Northeast. He also sat on the board of various rail lines who borrowed from the bank. Under your grandfather's tutelage, I had invested in the railways during their early years. Both of us doubled our money, then doubled it again. We lost touch for a while after Crawford moved here and started building the hotel. We reconnected after Preston granted a huge loan to one of the railways in which we were major investors, after which he and the funds disappeared never to be seen again. The rail line went bankrupt."

"He embezzled the money," Selene said.

"Other investors got caught as well, but your grandfather and I took the biggest loss. Luckily Crawford was never one to have all his eggs in one basket and I had followed his lead. Others were not so lucky. Families and lives were destroyed."

"And you both think he'll show up here."

"Preston despises self-made men like Crawford because he's not smart enough to be one. Crawford and I have a theory he won't be able to resist striking at us again, if only to make himself feel superior. Both of us in one town will be too much of a temptation."

Selene wrinkled her nose. "From what you've told me, robbery doesn't sound like his style. Wouldn't he be more inclined to try to swindle you?"

"Normally, yes. But he knows we'll be on guard against him making a move like that."

"But not on guard against me."

He could almost see the wheels spinning in her head. "I know what you're thinking, Selene. You are *not* getting involved. Which is another reason your grandfather brought me here."

She lifted her chin in that haughty way he was coming to recognize. "Afi doesn't believe I can take care of myself. What do *you* think?"

Beckett gave an ironic laugh. "I feel sorry for Preston if he gets too close. Or any man for that matter. Poor old Crawford has his work cut out to see you and your sisters married off."

"As you know, my plans for the future do not exactly align with Afi's."

Beckett nodded. Neither did his.

CHAPTER 10

Selene had no idea how he managed it, but the next day Beckett produced a compact safe that he installed beneath the false top of the bar.

"I guess I know now why you and Afi don't trust banks," Selene said as the two of them transferred the contents of the old safe in the office to the new one.

"Who said I don't trust banks?"

"I just assumed, given what happened with Preston—"

"My distrust of banks goes back to the war when my father had his money in a system that collapsed. Overnight, confederate dollars were worthless."

"How awful!" Selene's eyes widened. There was so much she still had to learn. Money seemed to be something Afi always had plenty of. The building block of power and success. She wanted the same for herself, independent of her grandfather.

"These days banks are more secure since the US Treasury instituted one banknote for the entire country." He checked the safe, locked it, and positioned the bar top back into place before they left.

Once outside, she took a deep breath. Music and joyful sounds filtered up from the festival. She had time to get some fresh air before the emporium opened. Just as she opened her mouth to ask Beckett if he'd like to accompany her, she spotted Deirdre Mathers. The woman gave a wave and crossed the street toward them. Selene's jaw dropped when Beckett waved back. Her feet planted themselves and refused to move. Beckett continued on until he reached the other woman's side.

"All ready?" he asked, crooking his arm toward the preacher's daughter.

A becoming flush tinged Miss Mathers's cheeks. "This is so lovely of you to escort me, Mr. Thompson."

"My pleasure." Without a backward glance, the two of them headed toward the festival. Selene stood staring after them. She closed her mouth with a snap. Wasn't this exactly what she'd hoped would happen? Beckett taking a shine to a woman not from these parts and going with her when she left?

Instead of following the couple to the festival, she turned toward the hotel. She'd barely set foot inside when Maia approached, almost as if she'd been watching for her. "Selene. Do you know where Beckett is?"

Selene blew out a breath. Last thing she wanted was for her sisters to think she never made a move without Beckett at her side. "I saw him headed for High Street." She didn't mention his companion. "Is something wrong?"

"I'm not sure. I'm reluctant to say anything to Afi until I have my facts straight."

Since anyone could wander through the lobby any moment, Selene steered Maia into the empty dining room and closed the door. "What's happened?"

"Carlos was on the second floor, making up the guests'

rooms. He was in Beckett—Mr. Thompson's room. He was smoothing the quilt when he felt a lump. He found this stuffed beneath the mattress." She reached into her pocket and extended her hand, palm up, holding a monogrammed handkerchief with the initials BT. When she opened the cloth Selene gasped. A gold locket and an emerald bracelet gleamed up at her. "Didn't you run into Beckett wandering the hallway late one night? Claiming he'd heard a noise?"

"Beckett is not our thief," Selene said flatly. "Afi trusts him. Besides, guests' valuables were going missing long before he arrived."

"True," Maia said. "And neither of these are among the items hotel guests reported as missing. But what about the robberies the other night at the emporium?"

"News travels quickly," Selene said.

"I heard it from one of the staff. I hoped it wasn't true." Maia sank into a dining chair. "I don't know what to think."

If Selene wanted an excuse to think badly of Beckett, Maia had just handed her one. Problem was, she didn't want to think badly of the man. All she wanted was to see the back of him. Once he bested his old nemesis, he had no reason to stay. Even if Preston didn't make an appearance, sooner or later Beckett would get bored and move along anyway. Maybe even with Miss Mathers. Leaving Selene solely responsible for the gaming hall, the way she wanted.

"For now," she said, "tuck these in the safe. See if anyone reports them missing."

"What about Beckett?" Maia asked. "If he's not a thief, someone is going to an awful lot of trouble to make it look that way."

"They are, aren't they? It would be helpful to know exactly who that person is."

Reaching the second floor, she heard the muffled click of

a door closing. It sounded like it came from the little library where she and Beckett had their card lesson. She exhaled sharply. Was every nook and cranny of the hotel fated to remind her of Beckett?

She approached to find the door, normally left open in invitation to the guests, tightly closed. She pressed her ear to the panel, but heard nothing. There was no reason in the world she shouldn't check to see why the door was closed.

She flung the door open and stepped inside.

A woman seated at the writing desk near the window turned her way questioningly.

"Lila," Selene said. "I didn't mean to disturb you. I was surprised to see the door closed, is all." She looked past Lila at the stack of papers on the desk before her.

Lila made a half-apologetic expression. "I didn't think anyone would mind. Our house is so close to the festival it's too noisy for me to work, so I tucked myself up here where it's quiet."

Right. Bolton's wife fancied herself some sort of novelist. "How is the book coming?" Selene said.

"I'm nearly finished," Lila said. "I must say this hotel was marvelous inspiration for the setting. What with the secret staircases and hidden tunnels—"

"Tunnels? Plural?" Selene interrupted. "There's only one tunnel. No one uses it because it doesn't lead anywhere."

Lila studied her in silence so long, Selene started to feel uncomfortable. "I would beg to differ about no one using the tunnels. I've been down there several times and there is definite evidence they are in use. The main tunnel, which leads from one side of the hotel to the other, has several branches, each of which leads to a different part of the hotel."

"Are you certain?"

"Here." Lila pulled a piece of paper forward. "I made a map because I use a similar layout in my book. A way for the murderer to move about unseen by anyone living upstairs."

"Are you saying someone could move about underground from one end of the hotel to the other without being seen?"

"Exactly." Lila nodded.

"Does Bolton know? Does Afi know the tunnels are being used?"

"Your grandfather told Bolton about them when we first arrived. He suspected it's how the thieves were moving around, and Bolton agrees with him. What with the festival starting, they were both busy with other things—"

"And you went exploring on your own."

Lila smiled. "Bolton is so protective. He would be horrified to learn I've been down there alone."

"Did you ever see anyone down there?"

"No. But like the heroine in my book, I got the sense of another presence nearby."

"You mean like a ghost?"

"Nothing so far-fetched. Just a sense of narrowly missing running into someone else. Someone who doesn't care to be seen." Lila leaned forward. "I keep asking myself, what would my sleuth do? Would she set a trap to find out who is using the tunnels and why? Even if it doesn't pertain to her case at the moment?"

Good question. In Selene's world, what would Jo March do?

She swallowed thickly. It was time to face her claustrophobia head on and overcome it. "Do you mind showing me what you found?"

"Not at all." Lila stood and stowed her papers into a

leather satchel. "I find it quite exciting. The research is more fun than the actual writing."

THE FESTIVAL WAS in full swing as Beckett and Miss Mathers strolled arm in arm along High Street. He'd been surprised when the preacher's daughter approached him to ask if he would be willing to accompany her to the festivities. In his experience, whenever anyone acted in a way that seemed totally out of character, there was usually something far deeper at play. Whether Miss Mathers was trying to distract him away from the emporium, or had some other motive, he figured there was only one way to find out. Selene's reaction to the situation only added to his day. The sight of her standing there with her mouth open would be lodged in his memory for quite some time.

A crowd had gathered around a magician performing a trick almost as old as magic itself. Three upside-down cups were on the table and onlookers tried their luck at choosing the one with the prize underneath. They watched as several members of the audience gave a try, only to come away empty-handed.

"How does he do that?" Deirdre asked.

"Why? Care to try your luck?"

"Oh, no. It wouldn't feel right." Her gaze darted through the crowd as if she expected the hand of the Almighty to come down and clip her alongside of the head for even watching others have fun.

"Wouldn't your father say there's nothing wrong since our magician appears to have enlisted the help of the Almighty?"

"Father might say that about a lot of things in life. I doubt he'd apply it in this instance.""

After watching a few more unsuccessful attempts, they continued on their way. "This is my first time at a street festival," Deirdre said, a wistful note on her voice. "I imagine you've seen all sorts of amazing feats in your travels."

Beckett stopped. "Who said I'd been to other parts of the country?"

"Oh, I just—" she flushed. "I assumed. I mean, a man of your stature and bearing seems far too worldly to have lived all your life in the same place."

Beckett ignored her blatant attempt at flattery. "Where all have you and your father visited?"

Her hands fluttered vaguely between them. "Here and there. No place worthy of note, really."

"Your father was never assigned a parish?"

She shook her head. "He says he always trusts the Lord to send him where he is needed most."

"And he decided Silver Springs is where he was needed? I'm surprised he's even heard of the place. Other than the railway station and the hotel, there's been little else here for the longest time."

"Father understood that's about to change. And with opportunity, comes opportunists. Men of little virtue. I think he was referring to the gambling hall."

Beckett ground his teeth, already regretting this outing. "Gambling in one form or other has become an integral part of society no matter where you are in the country. Games of chance have long been considered both moral and legal. Which puzzles me as to why your father would have an issue with the practice."

"He doesn't tell me much about his work."

"What about you? Do you get tired of being constantly uprooted?"

She gave a little shrug. "I have no other choice."

"Sure, you do," Beckett said. "Look around. The West is rife with a plethora of men who would happily trade their bachelorhood for life with a wife and family."

"Someone to share the burden of working dawn to dusk every day on their farm or the ranch?" Deirdre said primly. "Marriage might seem a desirable state for men. It's less so for a woman."

"It sounds like you'd get along fine with the Crawford women. They feel the same way."

Deirdre gave a delicate shudder. "Please don't lump me in with those women. It's hardly seemly for a gently-bred lady to be in charge of a hotel or a gaming establishment."

Further down the hill they paused to watch a troupe of acrobats. The man hoisted a woman atop his shoulders where she stood, stretched her arms to the side, and maintained perfect balance as he walked about the circle of bystanders. Applause broke out.

A second man joined the pair. The woman planted her hands on the second man's shoulders, transferred her weight to her hands before slowly raising her bent legs. As the crowd watched enthralled, she straightened her legs and formed a wide V for balance. Meanwhile her partner turned rhythmically in a circle with her upside down on his shoulders.

The crowd went wild.

"How do you feel about that job for a woman?" Beckett asked, more teasing than anything.

"Totally crass and vulgar," Deirdre said with an offended sniff. "The costume alone. To say nothing of a woman flailing her legs through the air for all to view her private areas."

The male acrobat grasped his partner's forearms as she tucked in her knees and folded herself in half. He placed his hands on her waist as she made a graceful hop to the ground. Joined by the first man, the trio linked hands as they bowed to the appreciative audience. Sunlight glinted on silver as the audience tossed a spray of coins their way.

Deirdre turned to him. "I believe I've seen enough vulgarities for one day. Father was right. The entire festival is a pagan ritual, tied to false gods."

She turned on her heel and marched away, back ramrod straight. Beckett watched her go. Something didn't sit right. What was Miss Mathers up to?

Before he could ponder the preacher's daughter's motives, a carriage rolled past and stopped abruptly. A man jumped out, and waved the carriage on.

"Beckett. I thought that was you."

"Callan. What brings you to these parts?"

"One of my reporters sent a telegram urging me to get here if at all possible."

"Lyon," Beckett said.

"He mentioned your name and said I really ought to check out firsthand what you and Crawford were up to out this way."

Beckett doubted Crawford would be pleased by Callan Douglas's arrival. The man was near Beckett's age, a newspaper tycoon whom Crawford decreed had too much influence over the reading public.

"I don't think either of us knew Lyon was on your payroll."

"He's not," Callan said cheerfully. "He's a freelancer who sells his stories to the highest bidder. Lately, that's been me."

Beckett wasn't surprised. Callan had deep pockets and was well known for his country-wide legion of newspapers. Beckett figured the man had other business dealings he preferred to keep quiet about, lest the public found out he wielded more influence than one man ought to. It wasn't general knowledge but Callan's nod, along with his financial support, could pretty much guarantee a politician's success at the polls.

Which could all change once women won the nation-wide right to vote. Knowing Callan, he already had something in the works for when that happened.

"You heading for the hotel? I'll walk with you," Callan said. "I have to hand it to old Crawford. From what I've seen, he's pulled off quite the coup here in the middle of nowhere."

Beckett made a noncommittal murmur.

"I hear the new gaming hall is the place to see and be seen," Callan continued, rubbing his hands together.

"You know what they say," Beckett said. "Believe half of what you see and nothing of what you hear."

Callan clapped him on the shoulder. "Ben Franklin, right? Anyway, if that was the case, I'd have gone broke years ago. People need to be told that what they're seeing is the truth."

"You'll have a hard time convincing the folks who are here to watch the magician's illusions. They want to disbelieve what their eyes are seeing."

"Pah!" Callan made a dismissive gesture. "The general public are sheep. One of them jumps off a cliff, the others will soon follow." He stopped abruptly and stared up the street at the hotel. Even Beckett had to admit it looked impressive, looming majestically over the countryside.

"Does Crawford know you're coming?"

"Now, now Beckett. Haven't I always been a big believer in the element of surprise?"

Turned out the surprise was on Callan when Beckett introduced him to Maia at the hotel's front desk.

"I'm sorry, Mr. Douglas," Maia said when the man requested accommodation. "We are fully booked during the festival."

"I know the hotel business," Callan said. "You always keep a room or two in reserve in case of—"

"In case of what?" Beckett said, feeling compelled to help Maia out.

"Mix-ups. Misunderstandings." Callan flashed Maia what Beckett took to be his most charming and persuasive smile as he leaned across the desk in a way that caused Maia to take a step back. "Besides, your grandfather and I are old-time acquaintances."

At least he had the decency not to refer to Crawford as a friend.

"Callan, I'll wish you luck as I leave you in Miss Crawford's capable hands." Maia shot him a look that made him feel bad foisting the man on her, but he had more pressing things to deal with.

He unlocked the door to the emporium, relieved to see Selene had taken heed of his suggestion not to be here alone. As he approached the office he stopped and stared. This morning, after he brought in the safe, he had tucked a matchstick between the door and the frame, knee high and out of sight. The stick was gone. He looked over his shoulder. Someone had been inside the office while he was at the festival.

CHAPTER 11

Selene made her way across the emporium to where Beckett was talking to a tall, dark-haired man. His companion was well-dressed and exuded an air of confidence that rivaled Beckett's. She stopped an arm's length away. "Good evening, gentlemen." A frown crossed Beckett's face so quickly she almost wondered if she'd imagined it.

"Beckett," said the other man. "Please introduce me to whom I assume is another of the lovely Misses Crawford."

"Selene Crawford, meet Callan Douglas."

"Mr. Douglas. I trust Beckett has been a gracious host."

"As has everyone I've met since my arrival."

Beckett wore his best poker face. "Callan arrived unannounced and wouldn't take 'no' for an answer at the hotel. Your poor sister eventually gave in and installed him in the honeymoon suite."

Selene raised a brow. Mr. Douglas must be as tenacious as Beckett. "Maia does believe it's unlucky to have anyone in the suite who is not officially honeymooning," she said. "Our grandfather was against the suite from the beginning, saying it took up the space of three individual rooms. But she held firm."

"I regret to say it is wasted on a bachelor like myself. But I'm grateful to have a roof over my head."

"Yes, the festival has the town bursting at the seams," Selene said.

"Which I'm sure is good for business in your impressive establishment." Callan encompassed the emporium and her in his look of approval.

"Don't let us stand in your way," Beckett said drily. "Feel free to go lose some money. You can afford it."

Callan laughed and sauntered toward the bar.

Selene raised a brow. "You have some interesting friends."

"I wouldn't call him a friend, exactly. But it's best to not be on his bad side."

"What does he do?"

"What doesn't he do?" Beckett took her arm. "I've been wanting to ask you something. Did you come back here after we installed the new safe? Forgot something in the office perhaps?"

"You mean when you stepped out with Miss Mathers? Not at all. I haven't been here until just before opening." Her look sharpened. "Why?"

"Just wondered." When he started to turn away, she caught his arm.

"You never 'just wonder'. There's a reason for everything you say and do."

"You give me too much credit."

"For instance," her eyes fastened onto his. "If you were to stash some women's jewelry beneath your mattress, I'm sure you had a good reason."

He stiffened. His frown deepened. "What are you talking about?"

She pressed her lips together before she spoke. "One of the staff was seeing to your room earlier today. He found some baubles under the mattress. Wrapped in a handkerchief with your initials on it."

Beckett made a big show of looking over his shoulder. "Has the sheriff been called?"

"Of course not. But poor Maia really didn't quite know what to make of it."

"No wonder she acted a bit odd when I saw her earlier. Other than shooting daggers when I left her with Callan, she avoided my gaze."

Maia shooting daggers at anyone sounded wholly out of character. Surely Beckett had misinterpreted her expression. "I said I'd talk to you. See if you have any idea who'd want to frame you."

"Possibly the same person or persons who were in here after you and I left. Did the builder ever return the key to the front door?"

"He said he couldn't find it."

"Convenient," Beckett drawled. "More likely he sold it."

Selene felt bound to defend the man she had hand-picked for the job of overseeing the building's construction. "Perhaps it was stolen. For that matter, how do you know for certain someone was in here earlier?"

"I used an old trick to tell if the office door had been opened while I was out. It had. And since it wasn't you or I, who was it?"

Her heart started to race. This was bad. Very bad. "Is anything missing?"

"I haven't had a chance to check closely."

She was suddenly grateful for their 'decoy safe'. "What is this 'old trick' of yours?"

"I'll show you one day when no one's around."

'One day' sounded vague and far into the future. Like she could be stuck with Beckett indefinitely. Which in no way suited her plans.

"Miss Mathers seems charming," she said.

"Um hm," he said, his attention clearly elsewhere.

"What?" she said, turning to see what had caught his eye now.

The room buzzed with the subdued hum of smartly-dressed patrons enjoying themselves. Chandeliers twinkled overhead of busy gaming tables. Across the room, whiskey flowed steadily from the bar to the shiny crystal glassware, to the guests' hands. The handful of ladies in attendance hailed from the high end of society. If they weren't the wives of the gentlemen they accompanied, it was no business of hers.

She turned to ask Beckett what he found so interesting, but he was nowhere in sight. She scanned the room. Blast! No sign of Beckett but that Markle woman was here. Selene would have wagered a bet of her own that this place was not Adria's dish of tea. If she was hoping to run into Afi, the widow was sadly out of luck. Her sisters had dragged him off for an evening of merriment at the festival with Bolton and Lila.

She was still troubled by Lila's tour of the tunnels. Fighting her claustrophobia, she had followed Bolton's wife below the hotel where Lila pointed out multiple passage-ways. They hadn't explored them all, but Lila had shown her several branches that led to the hotel's various wings. The ground was hard-packed as if well-trodden. Spent matches were carelessly dropped near the lanterns mounted through the corridors. At one point she spotted the stub of a cigar. As if someone had been down there waiting—waiting for what? Or for whom?

She circled the perimeter of the main gaming room. The lower half of the walls were paneled in golden oak wainscotting that matched the backbar. The upper walls were papered in a richly textured dark green and gold pattern. The colors of wealth. The colors of power.

A few patrons she knew by name, but most were strangers, none of whom gave her a second look. Not even when she stared at the carpet beneath her feet. Somewhere under this room was a tunnel. She gave an uneasy shiver. She'd told Beckett the tunnel couldn't be accessed from here. But what if she was wrong? Afi was always so secretive. Could he have arranged to have the tunnel completed without her knowing?

High time she had a little heart-to-heart chat with her grandfather.

Confident things in the gaming hall were running smoothly, she slipped into the office and shut the door behind her. Squatting down, she slid the wood panel aside and opened the safe. She pulled out the roll of building plans for the emporium, which had been created by some crony of Afi's. The same man who designed the hotel.

Out of habit, Selene locked the safe and slid the panel back in place, then took the plans to the desk where she unrolled them and anchored each corner with a paperweight. She studied the detailed pencil line specs of each room. No reference to the tunnel or a hidden opening. No hint of connecting this building to the hotel, below ground. She was rerolling the plans when she heard the lock click lock behind her.

She whirled. A man faced her, a black bandana over his mouth and nose, a pistol aimed her way.

He was medium height and build, with a nondescript black hat atop his head. He wore a black jacket buttoned all the way, its collar standing straight up. No vest or cravat visible, nothing that might identify him.

As she absorbed these details in seconds, she remembered Beckett warning her something like this might happen. Could she be facing Beckett and Afi's enemy, Preston?

"Open the safe." His voice was low and gravelly, an obvious attempt to disguise it. As he moved her way, her eyes flew to the door behind him. Locked.

She pretended to look around the room. "What safe?"

He waved the barrel of his gun toward the panel in front of the safe. "Don't play cute."

"The game is called Poker. The high-end games are on the far side of the hall. Which means you're in the wrong place."

"Actually, I'm not." Steely black eyes bored into hers. "No one else saw you come in here. No one will know what happened if they find your body in here later."

She studied his weapon. "One shot will send everyone running in here. You'll never get away."

He took a step closer. "There are other ways to ensure a woman's cooperation."

She repressed a shudder. The gleam in his eyes told her he enjoyed hurting women.

Crossing the room, she slid the wood panel aside, unlocked the safe and opened the door. "Help yourself."

Keeping one eye on her while holding the gun steady, he grabbed the small bundle of cash. "Where's the rest?"

"Things haven't been going well. That's all there is." As

she spoke, she edged back toward the desk. Her hand closed over a paperweight just as the sound of the door knob being rattled was followed by a loud hammering before Beckett called her name.

The robber took his eyes off her for a second. Long enough for her to hurl the paperweight, which hit him in the forehead and sent him stumbling back. Selene raced to the door. Her hands trembled as she fumbled with the lock. She expected to hear the robber's gun discharge, followed by the searing pain of a bullet ripping through her.

When she got the door unlocked the knob was all but ripped from her hand as Beckett burst inside, gun drawn. As he entered, he shoved her behind him. Selene braced for a shot that never came. When she peered from behind Beckett the robber was gone, the room empty save the two of them.

Dumbfounded, Selene gestured. "He was right there."

"I believe you. And now we know how he escaped."

"How?"

Beckett pointed to a trail of blood droplets. Barely visible against the carpet pattern, the red splotches led directly to the stone fireplace and stopped.

Eyes narrowed, he studied the fireplace's facade. When he turned to Selene, his gaze flitted past her to the design drawings spread across the desk.

"When were you going to tell me about access to the tunnel?"

Selene stiffened. It's not like she was obligated to tell him anything. "It was pure speculation. I wanted to gather more information first."

"Solve the puzzle on your own, you mean?"

She lifted her chin and faced his accusing gaze. "That, too."

His gaze probed hers. "You don't much like having a partner, do you?"

"No." She spoke before she had a chance to think her answer through.

It wasn't wholly true.

At first, she resented not only Beckett, but the underlying message that Afi believed she wasn't capable. Until she'd come to realize that Afi owed his success, in large part, to others. He wasn't afraid to reach out, to bow to someone's knowledge being superior to his. He surrounded himself with capable people and learned from them. She needed to do the same.

"Far be it for me to go where I'm not wanted." Beckett turned to leave.

"Wait!"

He paused, hand on the door handle, and half-turned to look over his shoulder. She caught her lower lip with her teeth. "I can't do everything alone. Not yet," she amended quickly.

He strode back toward her, his measured ground-eating steps reminding her of a predatory jungle beast she'd seen pictures of. A Jaguar. Sleek and black and menacing. It took every ounce of preservation not to back away. To stay put and meet him head on. He didn't stop until they were almost touching.

His eyes bored into hers. "Are you sure?"

She nodded.

"Not just put up with me the way you've been doing. No secrets. No sneaking off with your own agenda."

"It goes both ways," she said. "I've seen you in a huddle with Afi and Bolton. Your own little boys secret club."

He nodded. "It won't be forever."

"I'm counting on it," she said.

"The problem is—"

She fluttered her lashes. Waited for him to continue.

"The problem is, I arrived here with a very specific purpose."

"To help Afi best Preston. The emporium and I are simply the beard."

"It's more complicated." He hadn't expected to care about her. To care about this town. "And much as a part of me would happily walk out that door, to leave you flounder as you find your way, I made Crawford a promise."

She made a scoffing laugh. "There's that old boys' secret handshake again."

"Trust me when I tell you my business with Crawford has nothing to do with you or the emporium."

"Trust you?" she said cynically. "That's the problem with the world today. Men expect blind trust from the women. At the same time they keep things from us 'for our own good'."

"You have a point," Beckett admitted. "But let's just stick to a truce between you and I for the time being."

"And what about tonight's robbery?"

He pulled his timepiece from his vest pocket. "We've several hours before closing. I suggest we carry on with our normal evening routine as if it never happened."

Never happened? One more thing that was wrong in the way men coped in the world of business.

She indicated the fireplace. "What's to stop him from coming back? Or someone else coming through the tunnel any time they feel like it?" She could kill her grandfather for keeping things from her, but that was between Afi and her. Nothing to do with Beckett.

"Tonight's thief was already inside," Beckett said, almost as if talking aloud to himself. "And likely working alone. He saw you come in here and seized the opportunity, clumsily and without forethought. If he had an accomplice, I'd have been kept away with one excuse or another. But how did he know about the tunnel?"

"He seemed to know a lot," Selene said, recalling the intruder also knew the location of the safe.

As they spoke, Beckett approached the fireplace. He ran a hand down each side where the decorative trim met the wood walls. "There must be a hidden mechanism like the one in the hotel. It shouldn't take much to dismantle. In the meantime, Bolton knows some men. Discreet and trustworthy. I'll arrange to have one of them posted to the tunnel's entrance and another one here inside."

"I'd prefer to take this up with Afi." She'd be damned if she fell into a habit of relying on Beckett. Her emporium. Her problem to deal with. Although she had to admit Beckett's presence helped make what happened and how to deal with it far less daunting than a few moments earlier.

BECKETT WAS NOT NEARLY AS UNRUFFLED as he let on. Tonight's theft might not have resulted in much of a monetary loss. But it reinforced that they were the target of a relentless thief or thieves. If anything had happened to Selene—

He'd been frantic when he realized she was locked in the office with someone, and fully prepared to rip the door off its hinges. Once he knew she was all right, he'd been staggered to see she'd been poring over the building's plans. For that same purpose had sent him to the office, and he hated to think what might have happened had he not arrived in time.

He'd never considered himself and Selene as being

alike, but when they weren't antagonizing each other, they were shockingly compatible. She had to feel it too, judging by her reaction when he'd stepped out with Miss Mathers—Another piece of the puzzle that didn't fit. What were the woman and her preacher father really doing here?

He turned his focus to the latest rash of seemingly unrelated incidents. Not only were thieves plying their trade in the hotel, someone had gone out of their way to implicate Beckett. Was it the same thieves as those the other night? Or a different lot all together? What about the robber who escaped tonight? Was he somehow connected? Or was it all just a coincidence?

He thought of little else the rest of the evening, through closing and beyond. Back at the hotel, he had just pulled off his cravat loosened his shirt and splashed water on his face when there was a knock at his door. Apparently, this night was not yet over.

"Selene."

She gave him an uncertain smile. "You said you were a night owl. I took a chance you'd still be up." Her hair was loose and flowing over her shoulders. A shawl covered her shoulders. Although she was dressed in night attire, it was obvious she had not yet been to bed.

He crossed his arms over his chest and leaned against the door frame. "I thought warm milk was your cure for insomnia."

She glanced up and down the hallway. "May I come in?"

He stepped aside and waved her in. Rather than face him, she paced from side to side, clasping and unclasping her hands. Finally, with a weighty sigh as if a decision had been made, she turned to him. "Did you mean what you said earlier about me floundering without you?

He pushed a hand through his disordered hair. "No."

"Liar," she said, lowering herself into the straight back chair in one corner. The slump to her shoulders and the gaslight behind threw her features into part shadow, giving her a vulnerable air. She looked younger with her hair down. Less sure of herself.

He crouched next to her, balling his fists together to keep himself from running his hands through the loosened strands of her hair. Her head was bowed, focused on her hands in her lap. He placed one finger beneath her chin, raising her eyes to meet his. Hers were wide and troubled.

"What you're feeling is a natural aftermath of being threatened earlier."

She shuddered. "He was horrid. I could tell he wanted to hurt me. I didn't listen before when you told me to carry the gun on me at all times. But I will now. I swear."

"Are you saying you'll do what I tell you to for a change?"

"Don't let it go to your head."

"I promise." Feeling her tremble, he put his arms around her and held her against him. She sighed in surrender as she melted into him. The softness of her bosom cradled the hard planes of his chest. Even through his shirt he could feel the erratic beating of her heart. "Nothing happened. I wouldn't let it."

"Some things are out of our control." She toyed with the collar of his shirt. "What I came to say is that I value our friendship. The emporium is so much more with you there than if it was only me. You've helped me. It's my turn to help you."

"I don't—"

She placed her finger against his lips. "You're about to say you don't need my help. I beg to differ. This man who tried to ruin you and Afi, this Preston. You must tell me everything you know about him. So we can make a plan."

"I don't want you involved."

"Preston sounds far less dangerous than that man this evening."

He stood. "There is maybe one thing."

She bounced to her feet. "Anything."

"You're the face of the emporium. What if we put word out that you've run into financial difficulties, being a woman and all. That you're in need of a short-term loan until things become solvent."

"They are solvent," she said. "I've been diligent with my bookkeeping and—"

"I know that. But what if you falsify those records, make a second set of financials to be used as bait?"

Her mouth opened wide. "Cook the books?"

Beckett swallowed a smile. "You're familiar with the expression?"

"Of course. I've been doing the financials for the hotel since before it opened."

"Crawford didn't tell me that."

"Of course not. He prefers to downplay our skills. Says it will be off-putting for potential suitors if they think we're smarter than they are."

Beckett laughed. "That sounds like Crawford. Except he got one thing wrong."

"What's that?"

"Some of us are repelled by brainless women. And attracted to a female who not only possesses smarts, but knows how to use them."

"Are you one of those men?" Somehow, she'd sidled next to him. The room felt suddenly tiny with the two of them in it. He had to stop his gaze from straying to the bed. To imagining her there—

Her hands had hold of the placket of his shirt. He stared into her eyes and had the most unsettling thought that she knew exactly what he was thinking. Just like earlier with the building plans.

He went to move her hands, then changed his mind and anchored them in place, with his overtop. Her breath was like a warm river breeze. Her lips kissably soft. Impossible to resist.

"You didn't hesitate to kiss me before," she said.

"We weren't alone in a bedroom at the time," he said drily.

"Something tells me you don't need a bed to seduce a woman."

"Is that why you're here at this hour? Hoping to be seduced?"

"I was thinking more along the lines of a mutual, consensual tryst."

Which explained her lack of formal clothing. Beckett shook his head as he loosened her grip on his shirtfront and took a step back. "It's a bad idea."

She moved forward. "I believe it's an excellent idea. I have no desire for a dalliance with someone who will hang about afterwards like a lovesick puppy. You said it yourself. You'll be gone before long."

"Telling a man you can't wait to see the back end of him is not exactly foreplay, Selene."

"Precisely why this is so brilliant. Eyes wide open, no expectations beyond here and now."

He couldn't stop his half-smile. "You are a most unique individual. Which is probably why I find you so intriguing."

Her own smile widened. "I knew you fancied me."

"Is that a fact?"

"I even thought to take advantage of your interest. To use you in order to achieve my own goals."

"What stopped you?"

"The thought of being dependent on you or any other man. I have to get to where I want on my own merits."

"I'm sure you will."

"You mean that?"

"I do."

"Well then."

He couldn't stifle a faint twinge of regret as she headed for the door.

Once there she turned, as if offering him one last chance to change his mind. "Goodnight, Beckett."

"Pleasant dreams."

A faint smile played with her lips. "Always."

She locked the door, spun about and walked straight back to him, slipping her arms about his middle. "Please don't deny me this. There's no other man I care to have a dalliance with. No other man whose kiss stirs my soul, whose touch fires my blood."

"Believe me when I tell you there will be other men. Better men than me."

"I don't care about any others." She leaned back and pushed a wayward strand of hair from his forehead, her fingertips lingering on his cheekbone before caressing his face as if to memorize it by touch. "I am a modern woman, making my own choices, and I choose you."

He pressed a quick hot kiss to her palm, before allowing his tongue to lap at the soft skin of her inner wrist. She shivered, her eyes never leaving his.

"You seduced me with words that night in the library.

Admitted you have an awareness of me. Made me ache to feel your touch."

He couldn't suppress his smile. "I did that, didn't I?"

She leaned forward. "No more words," she said, her mouth a breath from his.

"Your wish is my command."

CHAPTER 12

Selene took Beckett's hands in hers and backed slowly across the room, not stopping until she reached the bed. Without releasing him she eased down onto her back, pulling him with her. He smiled as he freed his hands and placed one on either side of her, supporting himself as he arched over her, their bodies almost but not quite touching.

Their eyes locked. Neither moved. She could barely breathe for the waves of anticipation chasing through. Her fingers trembled as she reached to unbutton his shirt.

"Impatient little thing, aren't you?" In one easy move he was reclining alongside her, one elbow bent, his head propped on his hand. His free hand tangled through her hair, spread across his pillow. She rolled to face him. He smelled divine. Musky and fresh like the outdoors, his scent enveloped her, inflaming her senses, fueling her need.

Her shawl slipped from her shoulders. "Isn't this where you undress me?"

"All in good time."

His touch was as light as raindrops, as hot as noonday sun against her neck, her throat, her shoulders. When his lips replaced his fingers, she closed her eyes and sighed in pleasure. A needful pulsing spread from her bosom to her central core and she shifted, wanting, needing more. Everything he was. Everything he had.

His fingers pebbled her nipples through the light eyelet fabric of her chemise. His smile widened, obviously enjoying watching her squirm.

"Do you have any idea how many times I've longed to do this?" He touched her in a myriad of ways, his palms, his knuckles, the rasp of his nails, before he lowered his mouth and dampened the fabric with his tongue. She nearly rose from the bed, choking back her whimper of frustration.

He took his time with the row of tiny pearl buttons until at last, the edges parted, and she felt the whisper of air against her bare skin. How wicked she felt. How wanton. He didn't move, simply looked his fill. Beneath his admiring gaze her bosom swelled. Her nipples hardened in the cool air and turned a deeper rosy hue.

"Delicious." With one fingertip he outlined first one areola, then the second. She closed her eyes and enjoyed the fresh outpouring of warmth and dampness between her legs. At long last he lowered his dark head to her chest and suckled like a hungry babe.

"Oh!" Had anything ever felt so exquisite? The lap of his tongue, the warmth of his breath, the faint abrasion of his nighttime whiskers against her sensitive flesh. And yet, she knew there was more. Much more.

He stood and stripped off his shirt. Chest muscles rippled in the dim lamplight, while a light mat of dark hair dipped from his breastbone to ring his navel and arrow into his trousers. Magnificent. His taut planes, her curves, made to compliment and contrast.

He positioned her on the edge of the bed, hooked his

thumbs beneath the elastic of her pantaloons and skimmed them off, exposing her all together. Naked beneath his gaze, she had never felt so feminine, so desirable, so beautiful.

"I've never done this before. I'm not sure how I'm supposed to act."

"You're not supposed to act. You're only supposed to feel."

She exhaled heavily. There were no words for the cacophony of feelings trundling through her. Her heart pounded as he reached for her innermost recesses and found her damp with anticipation. Should she smile coyly? Offer up a maidenly blush? Even though he still wore his trousers, the front bulged with telltale signs of his arousal. She reached for him.

He caught her hand before she got there.

"Not yet."

He dropped to his knees, spread her legs and buried his face. Had there ever been a more moving sight than his dark head nuzzling her soft white inner thighs, kissing and licking his way up to where a tremendous pressure continued to build. She was so hot. He blew on her, his breath fanning already out of control flames before he brought his tongue to her, first her mons, then her inner petals, before making his way to the stamen of her womanhood.

She swallowed a scream as she shattered into a million pieces, one hand fisting the bedcovering, the other buried in his hair. He didn't stop but held her legs gently as he worked his magic, licking and laving until she lay spent.

When he rose and stepped from his trousers, her jaw dropped. He was truly exceptional, his cock jutting proudly from its nest of dark hair, a tiny pearl-like drop of liquid visible on the tip. She reached for him, marveling at the contrast of hard and soft. As his skin slid beneath her touch and exposed his velvety helmet he pulsed, flushed and rigid beneath her fingers. When she moved to explore this hidden delight, he sucked in his breath and stepped back a pace.

Had she done something wrong?

Apparently not. For he positioned himself at the apex of her thighs and introduced her fully to the delightful pleasures to be found between a man and a woman.

"PRESTON'S ON HIS WAY!"

Beckett looked up from his coffee cup as Crawford burst into the breakfast room waving a telegram. They were the only two up this early. Not that he'd gotten any sleep after Selene left his room early this morning. "Are you certain?"

"Confirmed by that detective I hired, as well as one of my people on the train. He should arrive the day after tomorrow."

Damn, they hadn't baited the trap yet. He hadn't even had time to bring Crawford on board about Selene being involved.

"I told you he wouldn't be able to stay away." Crawford look positively giddy as he took a seat across from Beckett. "Turns out he's in far deeper than we thought. A big score is his only chance to continue to draw breath."

Beckett had heard the same story from other sources. "Desperate men are the most dangerous."

"Maybe I should send the girls to Sulphur Springs until we've taken care of Preston once and for all."

Beckett chose his words carefully. "I don't think you could convince them to leave while the festival is on."

Preston deflated. "They haven't followed my directives for more years than I can remember."

"And let's not forget Selene is the face of the emporium. If Preston can be convinced that he's dealing with a female, in his mind an easier mark, he'll be more arrogant than usual. And sloppy."

Crawford's gaze narrowed. "You've given this a lot of thought."

"Selene wants to help. If we play our cards right, he won't know of any connection to you. But knowing you have a stake in this town, he won't be able to resist getting the best of you a second time. At least that's what he'll think going in."

"I won't have a granddaughter of mine in harm's way."

"Selene can handle herself. Someone tried to rob the office safe last night. She clocked the fellow with a paperweight and sent him running off with his tail between his legs." He didn't mention the robber making his escape through the tunnel. He needed to check out a few things first.

Crawford gave him his sternest look. "Why wasn't I told about this?"

"What would you have done? Stamped your hooves and lowered your horns in a threatening manner? Upset the patrons? Possibly even scared off Preston?"

"I assume you've already discussed this plan of yours with Selene? And she's agreed?"

"It was her idea," Beckett said.

Afi shook his head sadly. "That doesn't even surprise me. How am I supposed to keep those girls in line?"

"They're no longer girls," Beckett said deliberately. "They're capable women."

"Too capable for their own good," Crawford glowered.

"Why in tarnation can't they get married and become some other fellow's responsibility?"

"Any of them would make a terrific wife for some lucky fellow."

"This wretched festival is supposed to open the girls' eyes to a superior breed of available menfolk."

Beckett knew Crawford believed what he said, even if getting the town established and bustling was his main goal. "It's definitely put Silver Springs Junction on the map. To the point that the town is sure to eventually attract suitors who meet with your approval."

"I'm reassured to hear you say that. With any luck, we'll soon see Preston ruined and you can be off on your next adventure."

Somehow Beckett didn't find the prospect nearly as enticing as he once might have. Especially when Selene joined them looking positively radiant.

"I start to worry when I see you two looking thick as thieves," she said as she poured herself a cup of tea from the silver service on the sideboard.

"No thievery involved, my dear." Crawford stopped to press a quick kiss to the top of her head. "I'm glad you and Beckett settled your differences. He tells me you bested a would-be thief last night. Good girl."

Selene raised a questioning brow Beckett's way. "Yes, well. Beckett and I make a very good team."

"I'll let him bring you up to speed. I need to confer with Bolton about something."

Selene sent a puzzled frown after her grandfather. "What's he up to? And don't say you don't know."

"I don't know what he wants with Bolton," Beckett said. "But he's received word that Preston is headed this way."

He could see her attention piqued. "What do we need to do to prepare?"

"You? Nothing. Business as usual."

"Hmmph." Selene cradled her tea cup in both hands near her mouth. "Sounds like you get to have all the fun."

"Don't worry. I broke it to Crawford that you'll have a role."

She gave him a coquettish look. "My champion now, are you?"

He caught her hand in his. "From the first time I laid eyes on you."

"You hid that well."

"I had no choice. You were very convincing in your disliking of me."

She smiled into her teacup. "I always fancied I'd quite enjoy life on the stage."

Beckett laughed aloud. "I hate to tell you, but stage actors spend their entire careers following the directives of someone else. You're better off with the world as your stage."

"Quite right. That wouldn't suit me at all." She leaned forward as if to steal a kiss, only to be interrupted by the arrival of her sisters.

Beckett got to his feet and made his excuses.

"Something we said?" Chandra drawled.

"A smart man knows to retreat when he's outnumbered. Good day, ladies. Enjoy the festival. Selene, I'll catch up with you later."

SELENE SMILED A SECRET SMILE, remembering last night as she watched him leave the room.

"I see the way you're staring after Beckett," Minerva said teasingly.

Selene swung around in her chair. "You're imaging things."

"I've seen it too," Maia said.

"Chandra, defend me," Selene implored.

"Sorry?" Chandra was obviously with them in body only. What was distracting their baby sister these days? Had she met someone?

"Chandra's too self-absorbed to notice anyone else," Maia said.

"Well, *I'm* not," Minerva said. She turned to Selene. "Where did you wander off to for hours in the middle of the night? And don't tell me you were sleepwalking. Afi would have a fit if he thought you had a late night assignation with Beckett. Or anyone for that matter. But especially Beckett."

"Why do you say 'especially Beckett'?" Selene asked.

"I overheard them talking. Afi was telling Beckett that he wasn't the sort he wanted to see any of us end up with."

Selene strove to sound nonchalant. "Heavens. Was Beckett offended?"

"Not at all. The two of them had a good laugh about it."

Selene pursed her lips. Was seducing her all part of Beckett's master plan? One where she'd played right into his hand by going to his room last night. Hang Beckett. Hang all of them!

What on earth was she doing sitting here? She needed to talk to Afi about the emporium's tunnel entrance and find out what else he'd been keeping from her. Without a word to her sisters, she left the room and stalked through the hotel lobby where she found Afi and Bolton.

"Oh, good, there you are Selene."

Afi's positive greeting stopped her in her tracks. Her

KATHLEEN LAWLESS

suspicious gaze flew from one man to the other. Was this an attempt to mollify her, to keep her in the dark?

"I'll leave you two to your discussion," Bolton said. Selene wasn't sure if she was glad to see him go, or would prefer him here to buffer whatever Afi was about to drop on her. Because he for sure had something up his sleeve.

"Beckett says you know about Preston. And that you're willing to help."

"That's right."

We'll set things up to make it easy for you. In the meantime, I need your help with a different matter."

"What might that be?"

"I believe you met the Knightlys yesterday? The ones from the East with the Haberdashery business?"

"The couple who claimed they were robbed?"

"We've settled that issue. Their son is in town and I'd like you to show him around."

Selene opened her mouth to ask why one of the others couldn't have that honor.

"One business person to another," Afi said, his piercing look daring her to refuse. "Young Knightly and his wares are just the sort I want to encourage to settle here."

"What am I supposed to show him?" Selene asked, unable to shake her feeling that an ulterior motive lurked behind Afi's request.

"Paint a picture of what the town will be like once the festival is over. Let him know the potential. There are a few empty store fronts on that new strip near the station. Perhaps one of those would suit his needs."

Hmmph. Was Afi also hoping one of his granddaughters would suit young Knightly's needs?"

"There he is now! Mr. Knightly."

A well-dressed young man gave a hesitant smile, then

crossed the lobby toward them. Afi was grinning like a cat that swallowed the canary. "My granddaughter Selene just happens to be available to show you around this morning."

"Mr. Knightly," she said, gripping his hand in what she hoped was a no-nonsense business-like fashion. She'd wanted this. To be viewed as a success on her own merits.

"Make that William," he said, his eyes meeting hers in an approving fashion. She slid a sideways look toward Afi who was all but rubbing his hands together. Yup, lucky her. This 'favor' had been totally orchestrated for her to spend time with the type of man her grandfather considered suitable.

She smiled back. She'd take this up with Afi later, when they were alone. For now, she was simply a business owner encouraging a fellow businessman that starting up here would be a sound decision. "Tell me about your business back East."

"You're sure he won't recognize you?" Selene said, as she and Beckett stood with the many onlookers watching a puppet show across from the train station. In actual fact, they were watching for Preston to arrive.

"He only knows me by name. Remember, you are Miss Emmett. A woman in desperate need of backing for the emporium, started by her recently deceased father."

"What if he hears something different around town?"

"The plan is to make certain he doesn't."

Selene swallowed nervously. Everyone knew plans could go astray. "I can't believe you got Mr. Douglas and that reporter fellow to go along with you."

"Callan can't resist a good subterfuge. He knows Preston

slightly from years back. Preston will have no reason to suspect Callan of being less than on the up and up."

His words were interrupted by the whistle from an approaching train.

"Showtime," Beckett said.

How could he look so calm? Her nerves were a snarled mass of uncertainty and excitement as she watched Callan and Lyon standing just outside the station. Maybe the fact that Afi had allowed her to be part of the takedown meant that her grandfather was finally coming to accept that she was capable in her own right.

"And we're certain Mr. Preston received the missive from Callan?"

"One of Crawford's men delivered it personally."

Selene had no idea how the men had managed to communicate the various details for the past few days. Carrier pigeon, perhaps. Not that it mattered. The trap had been laid. The players were in place.

Beckett glanced over his shoulder. "There he is. Right on time."

From across the street, Callan nodded their way before he turned to greet the new arrival.

Mr. Preston was nothing like she had imagined. Slight of stature, clad in rumpled clothing, even from a distance she could see his shifty eyes never settled on anything for long. He looked relieved to see Callan. She couldn't hear what was being said, although she'd heard Callan and Lyon recite it for Bolton and Afi. Making sure it sounded natural and spontaneous.

"Don't stare," Beckett hissed, as he melted into the crowd. "You're watching the show, remember?"

"Right." She pretended an interest in the puppets' antics,

trying to ignore the butterflies bashing around her insides. Be calm. Act natural.

The watching crowd laughed as one puppet punched the other. Laughing was the last thing she felt like doing, but she joined in, resisting the urge to look over her shoulder and see where the men had got to.

Prepared or not, she jumped when someone tapped her on the shoulder. Warily, she turned to face Callan and Lyon. Seeing the hapless Preston between them, it was hard to keep her expression neutral. This man had stolen from both Beckett and her grandfather.

"Miss Emmett," Callan said, removing his hat. "Sorry if I startled you. The colleague I was telling you about has only arrived in town minutes ago, and is quite anxious to speak with you."

Selene avoided eye contact. "We can't talk here."

"I'm a busy man," Preston said with an air of importance. "I'm only doing Callan a favor by hearing you out. I never do business with a woman, and doubt your situation will see me change my mind."

Selene bit back a caustic response. Time to act desperate. She dabbed the corner of one eye with the hankie balled in her palm for that very reason. "I fear you're my last hope. Please say you'll meet me at the emporium in an hour. That will give me time to prepare. And you can see the property firsthand."

"Very well," Preston said, with a bored look. "While I'm here, I might as well see what all the hoop-la is about." He brushed an imaginary piece of lint from his sleeve. "Rather common things, festivals, don't you agree?"

After the three men left, Beckett reappeared and caught her hand in his. "You did great."

She gave him a satisfied smile. "You haven't seen anything yet." And neither had Mr. Preston.

Sticking to the shady side of the street where they were less likely to be seen by their quarry, they made their way to the emporium. Before long, the other players arrived and took their places. Her nerves had settled down, replaced by her determination to see this through. As she drew a deep breath, she caught Beckett's encouraging wink. It warmed her to her toes.

THE WAIT SEEMED interminable as the hands of the grandfather clock on the far wall crawled through the minutes. Selene jumped when booted footsteps, sounding overloud against wooden steps outside, echoed through the room. Stepping out of sight, Beckett signaled for her to greet their guests. He hated not being by her side, but it was the only way. Preston had to believe he was taking advantage of a helpless female who was all on her own. When she opened the door, Preston led the charge with Douglas and Lyon crowding in behind him.

"Mr. Preston. I was starting to fear you'd changed your mind."

Preston's glittery eyes devoured the gaming hall like a starving man in front of a baker's shop window. From the well-stocked bar to the glittery chandeliers to the roulette tables, his features tightened approvingly. "A man can't be too careful where he invests his funds. Your father was the driving force here, Mr. Douglas tells me."

"He was a gambler all his life." With a heavy sigh, Selene lowered her eyes. "A man consumed by his dream. When he passed away suddenly, I was left with mountains of debt. And no place to turn."

Preston swung a leather carpetbag onto the bar next to her. "It's your lucky day. I've been looking for an interesting investment. I know it's risky, but I'm willing to buy the place and pay off your creditors. If you play your cards right, there might even be a little nest egg left over that I can help you invest."

"I'm sorry." Selene blinked so rapidly, even Beckett believed she was fighting to hold back tears. "There's been a misunderstanding. I can't possibly part with Papa's dream. I just need a loan until I can turn things around."

Preston's mouth crooked in a rusty smile Beckett suspected was meant to put her at ease. "You misunderstood. I meant, of course, not buy you outright but that you and I would become partners. Still, a man has to safeguard his investment." He snapped open the leather bag and tipped it forward.

From his vantage point, Beckett could see the neat stacks of bills inside.

"I'll pay off your creditors. In exchange, I need you to sign the deed to me. A show of good faith you understand."

Beckett worried Selene might be laying it on too thick as she dabbed daintily at her eyes again and let out a tremulous sigh. "I know so little about these things. If you feel that's the best thing to do?"

"Now, now." When Preston reached as if to pat her arm, Selene shifted her arm out of reach. Good for her, even though Preston's eyes narrowed at the subtle snub. "Pretty little thing like you shouldn't need to worry her head about bills and business. Do you have the deed?"

"It's right here." She indicated a thick sheaf of bogus

papers Crawford had created. "Along with the monies owed. I fear it's a lot."

"You leave those pesky details to Preston. I don't want to see worry wrinkles marring that flawless brow. All you need is to sign the deed over to me. In exchange for paying off the debts, I'll add a proviso that the property returns to you once I have recouped my original investment. Along with a modest amount of interest for my troubles."

Beckett knew it was all a lie. The interest would accrue so rapidly the original debt would never be paid down. Preston would sell the place as soon as he could, all without parting with a red cent toward the bogus bills. He eyed the bag full of cash and wondered how many lives had been destroyed by the man.

"Shouldn't we have a lawyer to handle the arrangement?"

"Lawyers are the biggest bunch of thieves. No, ma'am. I happen to have a deed transfer all ready. It just needs to be filled in. Mr. Douglas and Mr. Lyon have agreed to witness our signatures. Isn't that right, gentlemen?"

Callan gave Selene a nod and Beckett wondered how he managed to keep a straight face. This farce was like a Kangaroo Court, only worse. He'd bet money it wasn't Preston's first time fleecing some grieving female.

"There you go," Preston said. "I've filled in the particulars of the deed and signed as temporary owner. All you need is to add your signature here." Selene signed her fake name, passed the pen to Douglas who added his name, followed by Lyon. Preston's greedy hands shook as he bundled up the original deed and bogus creditors' notes. "I'll take care of these over the next day or two and you can go back to having sweet dreams, knowing you did the right thing. Your daddy would approve."

"I'm sure he would." Before Beckett's eyes Selene's entire demeanor changed. She lifted her head and stood taller, her stance firmer. Her expression capable. "My grandfather I'm not so sure about."

"Grandfather?" Preston's brow furrowed.

"That's right. Afi," she raised her voice. "Why don't you come out and say hello to Mr. Preston?"

The look on Preston's face when Afi stepped out of the back room was comical. And it wasn't just Crawford. Bolton was with him, as well as a bounty hunter friend of his. Beckett stepped from behind the bar where he'd been watching, close enough to rush to Selene's aid should she need it.

Preston turned to face Callan and Ryder. "Is this some sort of joke?"

"Not by half," Callan said. "I believe you are acquainted with Mr. Crawford? He owns this establishment, along with the hotel across the street."

"You lied to me. I won't forget that."

"His granddaughter's signature is unfortunately not binding as she is not the owner of record. Crawford is."

"Hah!" Preston reached for the money. "I should have known as much. Not hard to see his filthy paws all over the place."

"Well, your filthy paws won't be getting any part of it." Callan stepped forward. "And I'll relieve you of this cash. Bolton knows several members of the Treasury Department who will be most interested in seeing it returned to its rightful owners. Here you go." He hefted the bag toward Bolton, who caught it easily before he turned to the man behind him.

"Along with seeing the money returned to its rightful owners," Bolton said, "I'd like to introduce you to Johnstone, a bounty hunter acquaintance of mine. Apparently, Johnstone knows some folks out East who are rather anxious to meet up with you."

Johnstone stepped forward and bent Preston's hands none-too-gently behind his back. His mustachioed grin revealed a middle tooth missing. "Favorite part of my job."

"It was so exciting." Selene paced the upstairs studio at the hotel as she recounted the day's adventure to her sisters. True to form, each one had gravitated to her favorite seat. Minerva sat at the table as if guarding her art supplies. Chandra was sprawled along a couch with her legs up and her back propped against the arm. Maia sat primly in a wingback chair. "Best of all, Beckett feels confident that hideous man won't get away with his heinous behavior ever again. The bounty hunter plans to turn him over to his victims before getting the authorities involved."

"You talk about Beckett an awful lot, you know. I didn't think you liked the man," Maia said.

"That's the even better part," Selene said. "Seeing that Preston got his just desserts was Beckett's real reason for being here. Now that's been taken care of, and he knows I can manage the emporium on my own, there's nothing to stop him from heading off on his next adventure."

The sisters exchanged a look.

"What?" Selene ceased pacing and faced them.

"He just extended his room stay indefinitely," Maia said. "Hardly the action of a man who has one foot out the door."

Selene plopped down onto the nearest chair. "Indefinitely? Why on earth would he do that?"

"Maybe he likes it here," Minerva said unhelpfully.

Selene straightened and turned toward Maia. "Did you ever ask him about the jewelry that was under his mattress?"

Maia laughed. "Why? Do you suddenly think he's a thief?"

"No, of course not," Selene said.

"He denied knowing anything about the jewelry. And found it troubling that someone is out to paint him as the guilty party."

"Maybe he intends to help Bolton trip up the real thieves?" Chandra said.

More likely he intended to continue to complicate her life.

"Anyway, no one has learned the identity of the man who threatened you," Chandra said. "Maybe Beckett is reluctant to leave you alone at the emporium with a maniac like that still at large."

"Beckett is not responsible for my safety." She felt the reassuring weight of her pistol in her skirt pocket. "Did you three start carrying a gun like I suggested?"

One by one they shook their heads.

"You're being foolhardy," Selene said as she stood. "Someone is using the tunnels for no good. Until we find out who and why, none of us are safe. Not even in our own beds."

"I went through the tunnels myself with the guard Afi hired," Maia said. "There's no further signs that anyone has been down there."

"You can't post a guard at every entry point," Selene said. "You'd have more guards than guests in the hotel."

"You're exaggerating as usual," Minerva said.

Chandra stretched and rose. "But she does have a point. It's a little creepy to think someone has been skulking around down there."

"Do we believe Afi when he says he all but forgot about the tunnels? He seemed surprised to find out how well-used they appeared to be," Selene said.

"You know Afi. Always trying to protect us, Minerva said, with a faint tinge of bitterness in her tone.

"Did you dismantle the entry point in your office at the emporium?" asked Maia.

"For now," Selene said. "Although it could come in handy at some point in the future."

"I'd love to know how that fellow who attacked you knew about the tunnel, let alone how to open it from your office." Minerva asked.

So would she. That missing piece of the puzzle could be the reason for Beckett's extended stay in Silver Springs Junction.

CHAPTER 13

"Tell me." Bolton finally got Crawford alone to ask the question that had been top of his mind. "What made you so certain Preston would show up here?"

Crawford gave a little half-smile. "It's all part of an ongoing plan, stretching back years."

Lord help them all! "Why do I have the feeling you have any number of schemes set to hatch all over the country?"

"You give me far too much credit." Crawford straightened. "Anyway, dealing with that cretin is behind us. Can we move on to matters at hand?"

Bolton eyed his old friend. What now? He liked Silver Springs Junction and his wife Lila loved having the Crawford sisters as her surrogate family. But being at Crawford's beck and call had no place in his future ambitions. "I've put word out that the festival will be an annual event. Expect next year to be bigger and better. And the emporium is already making quite the name for itself. It was a good move getting Beckett involved, even if him being here was to help trip up Preston."

Crawford nodded. "Beckett and I were united in our

determination to stop that toad. He had as much, if not more at stake than I did. I grow weary of waiting to see gentlemen of substance courting the girls."

"I told you from the outset you'd be better served enlisting the services of a matchmaker."

"The girls would never go along with anything of the sort. A show of interest has to look like a natural happenstance. Cupid's arrow or some such romantic poppycock."

"I'll leave that for you. As of now, it's far more critical we learn the identity of the man who confronted Selene at gunpoint and forced her to open the safe. It was sheer luck that the emporium didn't take a huge loss. I can tell you straight up, it was not the move of anyone who picks pockets. And I doubt the incident had any connection to the thieves who've been targeting hotel guests, either."

Crawford's bushy brows appeared to take on a life of their own. "Your wife was most intrigued when she discovered the tunnels. Who might she have told?"

"At your request, I asked her to keep her findings to herself."

Crawford looked unconvinced.

"Lila is hardly one given to idle chatter."

They both fell silent, Bolton swallowing a bubble of guilt. He wasn't being totally honest with Crawford. For Lila had recently confided that the detailed map of the tunnels she'd drawn as research for her writing had vanished. She wasn't sure if she had dropped it going from their home to the hotel, or if someone had deliberately taken it from among her papers when her back was turned.

Bolton had no intention of saying anything to Crawford until he knew whose hand the map had ended up in.

THE EMPORIUM WAS EERILY silent when it was closed. Looking up from her accounting, Selene's gaze strayed in the direction of the fireplace. Silly to feel threatened by a piece of architecture. The mechanism that controlled the opening had been rendered inoperable. No one was about to pop out and rob her as she pored over the accounts for the gaming hall.

Less than a week since they opened, and the numbers were impressive. Afi would be pleased. He'd balked at offering female guests a complimentary glass of champagne, but he'd soon come around, going so far as to compliment her on her idea.

Elbow on the desk, she rested her chin in her hand. So why this slight niggle of discontent? She played a major role in helping Afi and Beckett avenge an old enemy. She was the face of the emporium, an enterprise she had created from the ground up. She ought to feel proud. Yet, the business was part of Afi's holdings, while the staff looked to Beckett with any day-to-day operating questions. Had her expectations been unrealistic? Where was the elation she had expected to experience?

Her dreams: success, money, power felt as elusive as ever. No matter what changes had come about recently, men continued to rule the world. Why did that fact bother her more than her sisters, who seemed content matching their roles to society's expectations? Even Lila, Bolton's wife, had agreed to publish her female sleuth novel using initials rather than her first name. The publisher, a man of course, was afraid the story would not be taken seriously if readers knew it had been penned by a woman. Like Selene, Lila was well aware the literary world was home to a number of revered female writers, but she couldn't convince her publisher to risk it. As women tend to do, Lila had acquiesced.

And then there was Beckett. Why was he still here? Much as she'd enjoyed their dalliance and had no regrets, she didn't see herself as one of those women to casually take a lover. Had she known he planned to stick around a while, she never would have gone to his room that night.

Hah! Try another one. She craved his touch and his company, even now. Which is why her life would be better once he was out of sight, out of mind.

Her spine stiffened at the sound of someone moving about in the main hall. She immediately rose and took out her pistol before she tiptoed over to stand behind the door, which she'd deliberately left ajar. She peered through the crack between the door and the frame as masculine footsteps crossed the room. Whoever it was, they weren't trying to be quiet.

"Selene. Selene are you in here?"

Beckett.

She relaxed and tucked the pistol back into her pocket. "In the office."

As he appeared in the doorway, his gaze went from her to the desk, piled with accounting books.

"Sorry to interrupt." He raised a brow. "Good news?"

"So far, we've surpassed my original projections," she said.

"I told you I thought you were being too conservative."

"Better to have Afi pleasantly surprised than disappointed."

A funny look came over his face, too quick for her to tell what he was thinking. Did he know something she didn't? Something about Afi and his expectations for the emporium? Was she being excluded from the 'old boys' club one more time?

"Can I drag you away for a bit?"

Her heart leapt. Back to his room? A daylight encounter sounded deliciously naughty, and just the right distraction, for as a ploy to keep her thoughts at bay, doing the accounts hadn't helped. "Are your intentions honorable?"

Beckett gave his head a rueful shake, a half-smile making its appearance. "The purest. There's something I want to show you."

She swallowed her disappointment. "Another surprise?"

He buried his hands in his trouser pockets and rocked back on his heels. "Aren't you the girl who claims to not like surprises?"

Was she still that girl? The girl who didn't like surprises would resent the interruption. Not be delighted for the excuse to spend time with him. Even in the company of others.

"Let me just tidy up here." His eyes followed her every move, heating her blood and making her feel clumsy as she straightened her accounts into a neat file and placed them inside the safe before she locked it.

Out in the street, she made a show of craning her head this way and that. "No new signs?" It was said tongue-in-cheek, and elicited the response she'd hoped for. His smile churned up her insides, a combination of indulgence, patience, and understanding. Without trying, he filled that dissatisfied hollow inside her and took away her earlier feelings of being excluded.

"Fancy a bite?" he asked as they started toward the medley of festival sounds that filled the air.

"Everything smells so good." Each day the trains brought

more food vendors and their rolling carts from all over. She hadn't expected the festival to offer such a wide array of food choices, many from other cultures and unfamiliar to her. She sniffed the air, picking up a heady aroma of spices that she couldn't name. "I'd like something I haven't tried yet."

"I admire that about you. You're always willing to try new things. How about a couple of fresh oysters to start?"

Oysters? Was he serious? Once out of their shell, the creatures looked totally slimy and disgusting. Still, she recognized a challenge when she heard one. "Why not?"

He ordered from a man behind a wheeled cart piled high with the delicacy. "A few years back, it wouldn't have been possible to ship oysters across the country without them becoming spoiled," Beckett said. "But refrigerated rail-cars has totally changed the way we live."

And not necessarily for the best. She watched the merchant pry open the shell to reveal the ugly gray blob inside. He removed the top and she tried not to shudder as he extended a half shell her way. She eyed the offering on her palm with less than enthusiasm.

Beckett watched her, amusement twinkling in his eyes. "Go ahead."

"I'll wait for you," she said primly.

All too soon his was ready.

"Wait." He reached for a bottle nestled in the ice next to the oysters. "A little dash of this is just the ticket." He splashed a few drops onto her oyster and his, although Selene thought it would take a lot more than a dash of spirits to make her snack enjoyable.

Beckett slurped his oyster from the shell and smacked his lips with obvious pleasure. It didn't look like he chewed it. She stared at the thing in her hand, then glanced up at Beckett, who watched her intently.

"They say it's an aphrodisiac.

"Why didn't you say so before?" She tipped the shell against her bottom lip and drew the contents into her mouth. The oyster slid past her teeth and settled on her tongue. Surprisingly, it wasn't awful. A little briny, with a delicate hint of salt, it slid down her throat most pleasingly.

There could be something about that aphrodisiac aspect after all. "Delicious. It tastes so delicate."

"Hence why it's called a delicacy. Another?"

"Yes, please."

After they'd both enjoyed several more, Beckett said, "The oysters were my choice. Now it's your turn."

She surveyed the various carts lining this part of High Street. She almost suggested sweetbreads, but with her luck he'd probably love them. And she'd be stuck eating hers. She pointed to the pie cart. "A handpie would be perfect, thank you."

He purchased two beef pies and they started off.

"Not as adventuresome as the oyster," Beckett said, "but nicely filling."

He stopped her and turned her to face him. Unexpectedly, his finger traced the edge of her lips. "Crumb of pastry." He showed her on his fingertip before he popped it into his own mouth.

Something tugged at her insides. She ran her tongue across lips that were suddenly tingly and overly sensitive.

Next, he stopped at a beverage cart. "I think I'll have a beer. Fancy a lemonade?"

"Thank you."

As a one-man band passed, she marveled at the performer's ability to control so many instruments at once. She'd be lost before she even played a note. Balancing all the moving parts of the emporium was more than enough for her.

Beckett passed her a clear glass bottle of lemonade. She took a grateful sip, watching his Adam's apple bob as he drank from the beer stein.

"You said you had something to show me."

"I do." He took her arm as if it was the most natural thing in the world. "This way." Down near the station, outside the saloon, a familiar figure stood on an upended milkcrate, waving his fists in the air and expounding on the wages of sin to anyone who walked past.

"Preacher Mathers." She sent Beckett a teasing glance. "I wonder how he liked a reformed gambler stepping out with his daughter?"

"About as much as she did," Beckett said. "Look closely as he turns this way toward the sun. Just below the brim of his hat there's a deep red gash, quite recent from the looks of it."

"In the same place I hit the robber with the paper-weight," Selene said slowly, her mind whirling. "You think he was the one—?"

"He's one of hundreds of men in this town who own a black bandana. But he's the only one I've seen with a wound like that. Shall we go ask him where he got it?"

She tugged on Beckett's arm as he started to step forward. "I don't think that's wise. Then he'd know we're on to him. It would be better to catch him in the act."

"Selene." He sounded exasperated. "You can't keep putting yourself in harm's way."

"What do you mean?"

"We just got Preston out of the way. Now you're scheming to trip up the preacher."

She bit her lip. Beckett had an uncanny way of knowing

what went on in her mind. "Once his forehead heals, there goes any evidence of him being the one who had me open the safe so he could rob us."

"A forehead gash isn't enough evidence. He could have gotten it anywhere, and I expect he has his story prepared."

"I know! You should ask his daughter what happened."

Beckett laughed. "It seems unlikely he told her he got clocked trying to empty the emporium safe."

Selene turned her attention back to the preacher. As far as the passersby were concerned, he could have been invisible. If he wasn't trying to recruit a flock to save from the wages of sin, what was he up to?

"Watch him," she told Beckett.

"Watch him what?"

"Exactly! He's not even trying to engage with anyone passing by."

Beckett's eyes narrowed as he studied the man for several long minutes. "He's acting as a lookout."

She took his arm. "Now look over at the train station. On the bench outside. See anyone familiar?"

"Deirdre Mathers. Reading her book."

"Or pretending to."

Selene scanned the streetscape. Abruptly she sucked in her breath. "Come on. Quick." She didn't wait to see if Beckett followed as she beelined across the street, dodging horses, wagons and pedestrians.

On the other side of the road, Selene raced to where Lila stood in the shadows of the mercantile shop window. Lila let out a little squeak of surprise when they skidded to a stop next to her. Selene and Beckett exchanged a look. For it was obvious Lila was not interested in the array of household items displayed, but was using the glass's reflection to keep an eye on the preacher's daughter.

"Care to explain?" Beckett asked Lila. Selene admired his calm tone. He might have been inquiring about the weather.

Lila colored slightly. "Bolton has run into her a few times in the hotel, near areas she has no business being. Around the same time, my map of the tunnels went missing. I think she took it and was sneaking down there to check things out."

And if she'd shown her father, he could figure out which branch led to the emporium.

"My money's on the pair not being who they say," Beckett said. "Our friend the preacher appears quite interested in goings-on in the saloon."

Moments later a man left the saloon, stumbling a little as he headed toward the station. Mathers sent Deirdre a subtle sign Selene would have missed if she hadn't been watching intently. As the stranger drew near where Deirdre was seated, she tipped her book onto the ground. The man bent down to retrieve the book at the same time Deirdre leapt to her feet and skillfully helped herself to his wallet.

He returned her book, tipped his hat and continued on his way, unaware he'd just been robbed.

"Preacher's daughter my fanny," Selene fumed. "With her holier-than-thou act." She turned to the other two. "What should we do?"

"They're obviously crooks," Beckett said. "But I don't see any way to prove he was the one who confronted you at the emporium."

Lila chimed in. "Bolton feels the pair are simply opportunists, here for the easy pickings during the festival. Once it's over, they'll move on."

"And no one would suspect a preacher and his daughter." Selene turned to Beckett. "Something else about them is bothering you, isn't it?"

He gave a rueful smile. "You've got this bad habit of reading my mind."

"I hadn't noticed." She didn't tell him he did the same thing to her.

WHEN NOTHING else happened involving the Mathers, Lila left to share Beckett and Selene's suspicions about the preacher's fresh injury with Bolton, and Selene and Beckett started back to the hotel.

"You thought I didn't know what you were up to, trying to pair me up with the preacher's daughter when they first arrived, did you?"

Selene's wide-eyed innocent expression didn't fool him.

"Because I would have done the exact same thing, had I been in your shoes."

"My shoes?"

"Full of resentment at having some stranger foisted into my life and my dream, I would have been scheming how to eradicate them. Like encourage them to form an attachment to someone not from here." Her nervous laughter told him he had hit the mark. "I know you pretty well, don't I? Maybe even better than you know yourself."

She gave a disdainful sniff. "You give yourself too much credit."

He tucked her arm through his. They were surrounded by festival goers on all sides, but he felt like it could have only been the two of them. "I know people. That's how I knew something was off about the Mathers."

"Is that why you elected to escort her around the festival the other day?"

He bit his lower lip to stop from laughing. He knew his actions that day had not gone unnoticed. "One of the reasons."

"You think Bolton will see to it that those two get what they deserve? Even if we can't prove it was him who accosted me in the office that day?"

"Bolton seems to have the right contacts. Between him and your grandfather, I'm sure they'll find a way to deal with the pair."

"Perhaps then things will calm down. The festival will be over. You'll be off to someplace more exciting."

"I originally only planned to stay until Preston had been taken care of."

"I wish I'd known. I'd have been—"

"Less difficult?"

She drew herself erect. "I was not difficult. You were the one—"

"The one who enjoyed baiting you?"

She sniffed. "Even after there stopped being any reason for it."

"Was I baiting you that night you came to my room?" His remark stopped her in her tracks the way he meant it to. "Which begs the question, 'what happens now between 'us'?"

Her face could have been carved from stone. "There is no us. You're free to go."

"I don't think Crawford had any clue what could happen when he got me involved with the emporium. Knowing I'm not the type to settle down, he felt confident I wouldn't fall in love with you."

A faint flush stole across her cheeks. "That's a foregone conclusion."

"I'm hardly the man he would have chosen. Question-able past. Wanderlust tendencies. Yet, Crawford lost the toss. You see." He captured her hand in one of his, marveling at her soft skin, her fine bones. She was such a contradiction on every level. The fairer sex, but never weak. "In spite of everything, I've developed feelings for you."

He felt rather than heard her gasp and smiled to himself. Crawford wouldn't be pleased to hear this latest. The old boy had made no secret about wanting someone far more worthy to seek Selene's hand. But how did Selene feel?

"So the final card is yours. Say the word and I'll leave. Say the word and I'll stay."

She sucked in her breath. "Please go."

CHAPTER 14

He rocked back on his heels. "Still not able to be honest with yourself, Selene? I'm a bit disappointed." His tone implied her words had little or no effect.

"You shouldn't be. You've heard me state on more than one occasion how I want a life outside of the normal constraints of marriage. Since you claim to know me so well, you know I'm conflicted. Wondering, can I have my cake and eat it too?"

His eyes twinkled in that way she was coming to watch for. "I don't see why not."

"I suppose this is where you expect me to tell you that I, too, have developed feelings for you?" She blew out a breath. "It's different for a woman. I don't want folks to claim the emporium is only a success because a man is at the helm."

"I'd challenge a duel to anyone who dares misspeak of the object of my affections."

She tilted her head. "Would you have really left at my behest?"

"Only long enough for you to realize you miss me and can't face a life without me in it."

She laughed aloud. "Since you and Afi are such firm friends, I'll leave it to you to break the happy news."

His smile faded.

"What?" she said "You think he won't approve?"

"I'm certain he won't approve," Beckett said. "He has a very defined opinion as to the sort of man worthy enough for his girls."

"In that case, let's wait until after the festival wraps up. Given the event's success, he should be in a jovial enough mood so as to not make any rash decrees."

He raised her hand to his lips and kissed the back of her palm. Like every touch from Beckett, a tingly thrill swept through her. Her heart swelled and overflowed. She cupped his cheek with her palm. "I never dreamt I'd feel this way."

He pulled her close. "Neither did I."

"Well, well. How long has this been going on?"

Selene jumped. Chandra! She turned, hoping she didn't look as guilty as she felt. She had done nothing wrong. Except of course a public display of affection with a man to whom she was neither married nor betrothed.

Her first response was to deny whatever Chandra thought she saw.

But Beckett answered before she could.

"At least I'm known to the family."

Selene's focus shifted from Chandra to Beckett. "What's that mean? What are you saying?"

"I'm saying Chandra shouldn't jump to conclusions regarding you and I. Or others might be forced to draw similar conclusions as to her behavior when she thinks no one is around."

Chandra colored slightly. "Touché, Beckett."

"Will one of you kindly explain to me why you both are talking in abstracts and circles?"

"I feel confident your sister understands how certain situations call for discretion."

Chandra smiled and straightened. "I do indeed. I shall leave you two to continue what I interpreted as a heated business discussion regarding the emporium."

With that, Chandra sauntered down the hill toward the train station.

Selene's brow wrinkled as she followed her sister's journey with her eyes. "Why do I get the feeling Chandra is up to something? Something you know all about."

"If she has secrets, they remain hers," Beckett said. "That was simply an effective bluff. It wouldn't do for her to start a rumor that ends up catching Crawford's ear."

CRAWFORD HAD BEEN CATCHING wind of far too many rumors during the festival. He paced from side to side in his study. It was a terrible thing for a man to feel not only old, but also ineffectual. He stopped before the portrait of his dear, departed wife Carolyn, taking solace from his memories.

"I'm doing my best, my dear. The girls are a handful, to be sure. But I do believe you would applaud their high spirits and secretly encourage their independent ways. I know what you'd say if you were here. That it's not like me to be unsure of my decisions. But I'm hearing unsettling murmurs of Chandra sneaking about at all hours. Even her own sisters don't know where she is or who she is spending time with. Did I give them too much freedom when they were younger? I wasn't around much when Melanie was young. A move which left me woefully unprepared to raise four girls on my own. I wish you were here. You would know the right thing to do."

His out-loud thoughts were interrupted by a knock at the door. He crossed the room and opened it to admit Bolton, who hesitated on the threshold.

"I can come back later if you're busy."

"Not at all. Come in, please."

His friend scanned the empty room behind him. "I thought I heard voices."

"Only one voice." Crawford sank into a wing chair before the fireplace. "One lonely old man missing his dead wife, despairing of the future."

Bolton stood before him, one arm resting on the mantle. "A bit early in the day for melodrama, don't you think?"

"At my age, I feel I've earned the right to be indulged. To walk my girls down the aisle, then one day bounce a fat great-grandchild on my knee. Is that asking too much?"

"Matters of the heart are most unpredictable."

Crawford snorted. "You sound like you've been reading those books your wife is so fond of."

"Lila is partial to mystery stories featuring amateur sleuths."

"Mysteries or love stories. It's all poppycock and nonsense. Life seldom works out the way it's portrayed in books."

"True," Bolton said, shoving his free hand into his pocket. "It's also not as easy as it sounds to encourage the type of men to the area who would be of interest to your granddaughters. The festival and the emporium are a good start, but more of a foundation is required."

Crawford's look brightened. "I've come to that same conclusion myself. I've been going about this all wrong. To that end, my solicitor is on his way here to help me set up some things the way I ought to have done sooner."

"Such as?"

"My spies in the government tell me we're on the cusp of new federal regulations regarding business. The economy is changing. Survival of self-made men such as you and I depends on consolidating into larger economic units."

Just then Maia opened the door and announced that Mr. Jud had arrived.

"Show him in please. And have Flo fetch some refreshments if you don't mind. We have much to discuss."

SELENE PUSHED the pillow back to cover the linen closet peephole into Afi's study. It was true that eavesdroppers rarely heard anything good about themselves, but she had been unable to resist. As soon as Maia told her Afi was closeted in his study for a meeting with his solicitor she got a sinking feeling in the pit of her stomach. Afi was up to something. Something she and the girls weren't meant to find out about until it was too late.

Her thoughts continued to churn as she went upstairs to change into a suitable gown for an evening in the emporium. Her worst fears, that dowries had been attached to her and her sisters, hadn't been discussed. What she'd overheard was worse.

At the advice of his solicitor, Afi was arranging his various holdings in a complicated corporate structure which included much of Silver Springs Junction. Managers would be attached to each enterprise, the whole rolled into one umbrella company. A company which did not include her and her sisters.

Beckett was to be CEO of the emporium, which meant Afi knew he planned to stay. Bolton would become CEO of the hotel and the lands surrounding it. A group of directors would be appointed to oversee the railway and shipping interests held by Afi, Bolton and Beckett. Other items were also discussed, but Selene had heard enough. She and her sisters would have little or no say in their future. Worse than that, should anything happen to Afi, they'd be beholden to others for their very home and survival.

A quick check of her reflection in the looking glass told her everything she already knew. Her face was pale to the point that any color she might add would be too obvious. Her eyes were wide and troubled. The joy she'd felt earlier with Beckett was dashed to smithereens.

What if Beckett hadn't known his future was secure? What if he'd engaged her affections solely to guarantee his place here in Silver Springs Junction? Now and in the future?

If Afi had his way, Silver Springs would explode with growth and expansion. Something she and her sisters would have no part of. Afi would get his wish, for they'd have no choice but to marry. And nothing to fill their days but to become the type of boring, small-minded gossips she'd seen around town. Either that or busy themselves doing good works with the local church groups. Each option was as disheartening as the other.

She paused at the top of the staircase. With his uncanny sense of her presence, Beckett stood below. His admiring gaze caressed her. "You look exceptionally lovely this evening."

Normally her heart would give a gleeful leap at the way his eyes looked their fill. Then shift to a shiver of delight, a warmth in her blood, a longing for his touch. She didn't feel lovely. She felt disheartened and dispirited, as if everything she'd dreamed of and worked for: success, money, power, had been whisked away from her.

His look changed as she reached his side. "What's wrong?"

"Nothing," she said, avoiding his gaze.

"Nonsense."

She bit her lower lip. "It's not something I care to discuss."

His fingers were gentle as he tilted her head up to meet his gaze. "Whatever is troubling you, I implore you to share it. Burdens feel far less when shared."

She glanced behind her. "Not here."

Neither spoke again until they were the only two inside the emporium.

She turned to him. "Did you ever lose?"

"I beg your pardon?"

"In your gambling days. Did you ever lose something of the utmost importance? Something irreplaceable?"

"I'm happy to report I did not. I was never so attached to anything that its loss would devastate me. At least, not until I met you."

She studied him in silence. "Did your arrangement with Afi solely concern Preston when he asked you here?"

"Summoned me is more like it," Beckett said cheerfully. "Crawford is a master at creating bonds with others. And doesn't hesitate to use them."

She noticed he didn't answer the question. "So you had no inkling what he was really up to? His true intentions."

"Selene, speaking in riddles doesn't suit you."

"I overheard Afi earlier with his solicitor. Making plans to expand his empire. To restructure all of his holdings."

"Your grandfather is a very astute businessman, Selene.

If he is making corporate changes, he must have a good reason. The government is probably responsible, at least in part."

"The government?"

"I've known for quite some while that things in America couldn't continue. The time has passed for the economy to be soundly spearheaded by small ventures with sole proprietors. There's been too much economic crises leading to failures of small businesses."

"He plans to put you in charge of the emporium. Maia will no longer oversee the hotel. He already stopped Minerva from her dream of pursuing studies in Paris. Lord knows what Chandra has been up to lately, but he will no doubt kibosh that as well. Next thing he'll hire an embroidery teacher to keep us busy."

Beckett laughed.

"I don't see you taking up needlework, my love." He looked behind her. "Oh good. Here come the staff. I didn't want to leave you alone."

"Where are you going?"

"To talk to Crawford. Get this all straightened out. I know you won't sleep until you're assured you will not be displaced as the one in charge."

Selene sighed. She wanted to be the one to confront Afi, to demand answers and satisfaction. But it was very much a man's world. And she believed Beckett. Every bone in her body knew he was sincere. He cared more for her than for himself. He'd see things got put right.

"Very well. I shall anxiously await your return."

He pressed a quick kiss to her forehead.

"Will you tell him about us?"

"Not yet. I want him to see you deserve this on your own merit, not because you and I have joined forces."

She crossed her hands over her chest as she watched him leave. His words, his belief in her, touched her in ways she'd never felt before. Could joining forces with Beckett, rather than weaken her, lead to a fortified strength? A level of success she could never achieve on her own.

BECKETT WHISTLED as he made his way across the hotel's empty lobby. Selene was unlike any woman he'd ever known and required special handling. He never would have expected that this little junket to Silver Springs Junction would result in his meeting the one woman who constantly delighted, surprised and intrigued him to the point that he was willing to stay in one place. Falling for Crawford's granddaughter might well be the biggest gamble of his life.

He smiled. He never lost and wasn't about to start now.

The door to Crawford's study stood ajar. He knocked and pushed it open with one motion. A single beam of lamplight did nothing to dispel the shadows in the corners. And in no way prepared him for one shadow to separate from the rest. From the corner of his eye, too late, he saw the brass poker coming in for a direct hit.

CHAPTER 15

For the next hour and a half, Selene alternated between delight that Beckett chose to confront Afi, and concern when he didn't return. Were the pair in the midst of some man-talk huddle excluding women? How long could their conversation possibly take? Even if he and Afi decided to toast the future, it wasn't like Beckett to leave her here on her own.

She glanced around. Ironic, really. Alone in the midst of a crowd. Yet, without Beckett, she did feel alone. More alone than ever in her life. A loneliness that couldn't be dispelled by the company of her sisters.

She and Beckett shared such a special connection. He understood how she felt, and rather than belittle her or force her to deny those desires, he encouraged her. It was a truly rare experience.

Another hour crawled past. And with it a foreboding dread. Something was wrong! She fetched her shawl and stopped by the bar for a quick word with the man behind it, before she rushed across the street toward the hotel.

She hadn't reached the front door, when she heard a

familiar voice echoing up the drive. She turned to see Afi's unmistakable snow-white head shimmer in the moonlight. He was in the company of several other men and feeling no pain, judging by his unsteady gait and off-key singing.

She blew out a breath. Menfolk! At the festival celebrating, and leaving the women to keep the home fires burning. Or in her case, to keep the emporium fires banked. She crossed her arms and waited as they weaved their way toward her. Beckett was not among them.

"What have you done with Beckett?" she demanded.

Afi's song died on his lips. "Selene. Is that you? We've had a very busy night."

"So I see. Where's Beckett?"

Bolton stepped forward, sober from the looks of him. "Isn't he at the emporium with you?"

She shook her head. "He left hours ago. Came here to speak with Afi. Told me he wouldn't be long."

Afi appeared to sober. "I haven't seen him."

Selene recoiled. "He's been gone for hours. Is it possible he went to look for you at the festival and you missed each other?" Even as she spoke, she knew the idea was preposterous. Beckett would not wander around the festival for hours on his own.

"I'll get the spare key to his room from Maia and see if he's there," Bolton said.

"I'm coming too," Selene said.

Bolton's voice was firm but gentle. "Stay here with Callan and your grandfather, Selene."

"Come inside," Afi said. "I'm sure there's a perfectly sound explanation. Perhaps he fell asleep."

Asleep! Selene opened her mouth then closed it, reluctant to speak her mind in front of Callan. While he had helped with Preston, she was unsure if he was Afi's rival or coconspirator.

They had barely stepped inside the lobby when Bolton returned. Alone. He directed his words to Selene. "I'm not sure how to tell you this. But he's gone."

"Gone where?"

"Cleared out. He left you a note."

Bolton passed her a folded sheet of paper with her name scrawled across the front. "Have you read it?"

He shook his head.

Unsteadily, she unfolded the single page and crossed to a gaslight sconce so she could read what it said.

Sorry to leave so suddenly. Something came up. B

Woodenly she passed the note to Bolton. Afi read over the other man's shoulder.

"There, you see," Afi said. "Nothing to worry about."

Bolton must have thought different. "Has he done this sort of thing before, Crawford? Left unexpectedly?"

"More than once," Afi said.

"So, it's not out of character."

"Beckett and I both knew there was nothing to hold him here indefinitely. With the festival ending tomorrow and the emporium full steam ahead, it was only a matter of time until he grew bored and moved on."

Selene heard Afi as if from a great distance away. It simply wasn't true. It couldn't be. She turned abruptly. "I'd best get back for closing." The words tasted like dust in her mouth. She'd never closed without Beckett. He'd warned her not to be caught alone. What if thieves had incapacitated him in order to set up a robbery, knowing full well she'd be alone after the doors closed?

She patted her pistol where it rested heavily in her pocket. First things first. Finish up the evening, send the staff on their way, and secure all cash in the safe. And lord help anyone who got in her way or tried to stop her.

Minerva stuck her head into Maia's office at the rear of the hotel. "I'm worried about Selene."

Maia put aside her pen and beckoned Minerva to enter. "Where is she?"

"She's upstairs. Poor thing tried to be quiet, but she sobbed most of the night and finally fell asleep around dawn."

Maia pressed her lips together. "I know Beckett left on short notice. I found a note apologizing for his sudden departure, along with the money to cover his stay. But I wouldn't have expected Selene to take him leaving so hard. She didn't even like the fellow."

"That's not true." Chandra strolled into the office in time to hear part of what they were discussing. "I came across the two of them yesterday at the festival looking quite cozy."

"Define cozy," Maia said.

"You know standing close, gazing adoringly into each other's eyes."

Maia glanced over to Minerva. "Has she spoken to you about him at all? I wonder if he made overtures and promises, then left her high and dry. He seems the type."

Chandra bristled. "What would you know about a type?"

"Probably less than you," Maia drawled. "Given your schedule of late evenings and frequent long absences from the hotel."

"My business," Chandra said with a sniff, pushing past Selene who was on her way in.

"No wonder my ears were burning." Selene looked accusingly from one sister to the other.

Minerva felt herself flush. "I could tell you were upset last night."

Selene straightened. "Last night I was upset. Today, I'm mad and seriously disappointed."

"Girls, girls." Afi poked his head around the open door. "The entire hotel can tell that someone is mad."

Selene dragged him inside. Minerva jumped when she slammed the door. "Most of all I'm mad at you."

Afi blinked innocently at her. "What did I do?"

"Everything!" She met the curious look from the others. "Starting with undermining our importance in your affairs."

Afi bristled, his brows practically jumping into his hairline. "Now see here young lady. That's no way to speak to your grandfather. I'm not sure what you think you know—"

"I know you're making significant changes to the structure of your business interests. Each branch to be headed by a male. Including this hotel." She punctuated her words with a pointed look in Maia's direction.

Maia turned to their grandfather. "Afi?"

Afi looked like he'd rather be anyplace than facing a firing squad of his granddaughters. "The world is changing rapidly, girls. So is commerce, industry, the way people conduct business. I won't be here forever. I needed to leave my affairs in capable hands."

"More capable than us, your family?" Selene said.

Minerva and Maia both nodded in agreement.

Afi reached for a chair and folded into it, as if it was suddenly too much effort to stand.

"If she were here, your grandmother would say the same

thing. She was a woman ahead of her time. But I'm concerned that once I'm no longer around, the vultures will descend and single you out, based on the fact you're female. I wanted to spare you that. Plus, I'm old-fashioned enough to believe that a home and family is a woman's greatest accomplishment."

"As Charlotte Bronte so succinctly expressed through her heroine Jane Eyre, 'it is narrow-minded in their more privileged fellow-creatures to say that they ought to confine themselves to making puddings and knitting stockings'." Minerva flushed with pride as her sisters applauded. Afi hung his head.

"Jud has yet to draw up the final papers. I'm willing to sit down together and come to a reasonable compromise. Something that will keep you all as active in the business as you want to be, without your roles being a burden."

Minerva looked from Selene to Maia. "I think that sounds reasonable. Are all in accord?"

The other two nodded.

"I'm glad that's settled." Selene said. "We need to turn our energies to Beckett's disappearance." She leveled an accusing glare at Afi. "Why would he leave just as you were about to give him sole control of the emporium?"

"You don't know Beckett the way I do. Plus, I hadn't told him my plans yet. As far as he knew, his work here is done and it's time for him to move on. That's what he usually does. Gets his gambling fix in ways other than the gaming tables."

"I know Beckett well enough to know he had no plans to leave. His room was booked into the foreseeable future."

Afi's face softened. "Did he make you promises, Selene? He's not the type to settle down, you know. Too much of the gambler and the wanderlust. Driven by passion alone."

"And if I became his passion?" Selene said.

Minerva's gasp echoed Maia's. Afi looked shattered. You could have cut the tension with a knife. Everyone jumped at a loud rapping at the door.

"Come," Afi barked.

Bolton stepped inside. "Oh, good. You're all together."

"It's not a good time," Afi said.

"This won't wait," Bolton said. "I learned through my railway contacts that there was only one train through here after midnight last evening. And Beckett was not on board."

Selene turned accusing eyes to her family. "What did I tell you?"

Afi looked befuddled. "Then where is he?"

BECKETT BLINKED as he slowly came to. His head ached something fierce and he had no idea how long he'd lain on the dirt floor of what appeared to be an abandoned cabin. The windows were blacked out, making it impossible to judge whether it was day or night. The dirty rag in his mouth had long since sucked up every last drop of moisture. His limbs were cramped, his wrists and ankles raw from the tight ropes that bound them.

Was this his destiny? To spend his last hours in this hell-hole?

What would Selene make of his disappearance? Would she think he'd lied to her; become restless and moved on? He wouldn't blame her. He'd hardly given her much assurance that he meant what he said. How did one tell a woman she was the most important thing in one's life, and have her believe it?

Hinges squeaked behind him. The door opened and he

turned his head fast enough to see a crack of dusky sky before it slammed shut. He'd been here all night and most of the day.

"Well, well. Look who's finally stirring." Mathers made no effort to disguise his voice, which meant he didn't care that Beckett knew who had snatched him up. Not a good sign.

"I bet he's thirsty," said a softer, female voice. Deirdre Mathers bent over him. "Thirsty, Beckett?"

He blinked rapidly.

"Too bad." She spat near his feet before she rose. "Lap that up. If you can." She turned to Mathers. "It's nearly dark. How much longer?"

"We'll wait till the fireworks start. They'll cover the smell of smoke until it's too late."

Beckett sent a questioning look to the pair.

"Why?" Mathers said. He turned to Deirdre. "He wants to know why he's here."

"Should we tell him? Or let him die wondering."

"No harm in him knowing." He sent Beckett a malicious look. "You destroyed my brother."

"Preston was your half-brother," Deirdre corrected. As if semantics mattered.

"My only brother. He refused to listen and stay away, even after I told him you and Crawford were up to no good where he was concerned."

Deirdre turned to Mathers with a satisfying smile. "One down. How many more to go?"

Blood roared in Beckett's ears. He hadn't seen this coming. None of it. He needed to get out of here. To warn Crawford and the girls they were the couple's next targets.

AFTER MAIA SHOOED them from her office, Selene waylaid Bolton in the far corner of the lobby, away from prying eyes. "How can a man and his belongings simply disappear?"

"Men who deliberately choose to disappear usually know what they're doing, and are very good at it," Bolton said.

Of course. As a former bounty hunter, Bolton would know all the ins and outs of men looking to disappear.

"Walk me through it again," Bolton said. "You and Beckett are at the emporium. Why did he come back to the hotel?"

"He did it for me, after I told him about Afi restructuring his business holdings. I overheard Afi talking to his solicitor, you see. Beckett wanted to speak with Afi on my behalf before things were finalized." She shrugged. "Man to man."

"Yet Crawford wasn't here," Bolton said. "He was at the festival with Callan and myself. Would Beckett have gone looking for him?"

Selene gave her head a jerky shake. "He wouldn't leave me at the emporium to close things down alone. He would have come back."

"Except he couldn't. Which means he was snatched up almost immediately."

"In the hotel, or in the street?" Selene asked.

"Too many witnesses in the street. Which means—" Bolton strode down the hall toward Afi's study, Selene at his heels.

"Sorry to interrupt," Bolton said, as he barged in on Afi who was in a huddle with his solicitor. "Selene and I were wondering. Did you happen to notice anything out of place when you came in here earlier?"

"Such as?" Afi said, looking from her to Bolton, a frown on his forehead.

"Signs of a struggle, perhaps."

"Nothing amiss." He frowned. "Except the fireplace poker had fallen from its stand."

Selene and Bolton rushed to the fireplace. Her heart sank even before Bolton confirmed her worst fears.

"Blood," he announced, after taking the poker over to the window so he could study it in the fading daylight.

"How could someone drag Beckett out of the hotel against his will?" Selene wondered aloud. "And empty out his room? There's a huge risk of being seen."

Afi cleared his throat. "You think Beckett was snatched from this room?"

"He came looking for you," Selene said, her words drowned out by Bolton.

"It's starting to look that way."

Afi rose slowly as if his joints ached. He shuffled over to the fireplace and touched a spot. The panel slid aside, just like the one in her office at the emporium. Selene pushed past Bolton. Dark, dried drops of blood were visible inside the tunnel's entrance.

She turned to her grandfather. "Afi, this is a different tunnel."

"This one was built first," her grandfather said. "It's the only one that leads to an outside exit," He shrugged. "In case."

"In case what?" his solicitor asked.

"A man in my position makes the occasional enemy along the way. It seemed prudent to have a way out should I ever need one."

"So whoever it was must have knocked Bolton out and left him here while they went to his room to gather up his things and leave the note."

"That's pretty chancy," Bolton said. "Crawford could

have come back at any time. The perpetrator could have been spotted entering or leaving Beckett's room." He turned her way. "Selene, check with Maia. See if any of the guests left in a hurry."

Selene nodded. She'd far rather go trucking through the tunnel to see where it led, but more than likely Beckett and his accosters were long gone. She shot her grandfather a look on the way out. "Any other surprises, Afi?"

"I was trying to keep us safe. That's all."

A childhood memory surfaced. How they'd been schooled to run like the wind to the study if they ever heard the outside bell ring. This is how he planned to ensure their safety.

How many enemies had her grandfather made over the years? And how many more would show up looking to even the score?

CHAPTER 16

As she and Beckett had agreed before his disappearance, Selene closed the emporium early on the festival's last night. A few of the patrons were disgruntled, but most seemed content to take in the sights, knowing the emporium was here to stay.

Selene begged off when her sisters pleaded with her to spend the last few hours of the festival with them. How could she celebrate with Beckett still missing? The sheriff had been notified, but she had little faith in the law.

"You shouldn't be alone." Minerva swung from the mirror to face her.

"Run along and have fun. I'll be fine." Funny how a few days ago the emporium's success felt like the most important thing in the world. Now, without Beckett, it had no meaning.

"Promise you won't go out on your own trying to find Beckett."

"I promise." A promise she'd never keep if she had even the slightest clue where he might have been taken.

She swallowed thickly, recalling how much she'd

resented him at first. How determined she'd been to be successful on her own. How quickly things change. Everything she'd once considered important: money, success, power, meant nothing without being able to share it with him.

As she stared out the window watching dusk slowly soften the mountain's harshness, the stillness was shattered by a loud noise. Like an explosion.

Fireworks!

Selene rushed to the studio, opened the sash, and climbed out onto the roof. In their younger years, the girls often sat out here late at night, knowing Afi would have a conniption fit if he ever found out. But up here, closer to the heavens, where the stars felt near enough to reach out and touch, Selene always felt closer to her mother.

Tonight, the sky was ablaze with man-made shooting stars. Afi, always fascinated with pyrotechnics, had funded the career of a retired military man when he turned his talents to making fireworks. Afi must have had the fellow come to Silver Springs Junction to set up tonight's display. How like her grandfather to end the festival with a bang. Literally. To ensure folks returned next year.

Parked between the hotel and the festival's main stage was the fire wagon Afi had purchased last year. Pulled by a matched team, the conveyance was driven by two firemen and carried not only a huge barrel of water but hundreds of feet of hose and the latest equipment.

A faint breeze came her way, carrying the underlying smell of smoke. But not from the fireworks. A dark smoky cloud moved her way from the opposite direction. She scanned the horizon. Was that the faint glow of fire to the north? Fear lent her wings as she climbed back inside and raced down the stairs two at a time.

High Street was choked with people. Fascinated crowds gazed upward at the fireworks as she jostled her way through to the firewagon. She tugged on the sleeve of the driver, who appeared as enthralled as the rest of the onlookers. When she finally caught his attention and gestured to the north, his eyes widened. He yelled something to his partner and picked up the reins.

Selene clambered into the back of the wagon behind the driver and hung on tight as the conveyance careened in the direction of the blaze at breakneck speed.

THE FIREWORKS DISPLAY caught and held her sisters' attention the way Chandra had anticipated. Seconds after it started, she slipped through the crowd and made her way to the magician's tent. TJ was standing out back, face to the sky, his chiseled features highlighted then hidden in time with the fireworks.

She sidled up next to him. "I assume you've had the chance to mull over what we spoke about yesterday?"

"Some."

"And?" She strove to make her tone casual, as if she didn't care one way or the other.

"You'll have my decision tomorrow."

She huffed out a breath as she studied him. Why did she get the feeling he was enjoying keeping her waiting?

Overhead, the last sparks of the fireworks faded to darkness. Chandra hoped her plans weren't doomed to fizzle out the same way. She looked around. "Where's your father?"

"There's something going on at the hotel. I sent him as our representative."

"Oh." She'd probably known about the event at the

hotel, but put it out of her mind. Afi would be riled if she didn't make an appearance.

"Personally," TJ said, "I have no interest in seeing how the other half lives. But that kind of thing fascinates the old man."

"CHANDRA'S DONE IT AGAIN," Maia said, once there was a lull in the fireworks. "Given us the slip."

"She's always been irresponsible that way," Minerva said. "It seems unlikely she might suddenly change. To start and think of someone besides herself."

"Evening ladies."

Maia turned. Then wished she hadn't. It was that egotistical Callan Douglas. Along with that nosy reporter fellow who worked for one of Douglas's newspapers. She couldn't imagine why Afi put up with either of them, let alone gave them preferential treatment. Such was the world of men and business. A brotherhood she was unlikely to ever understand.

"Gentlemen," she said coolly.

"I'd like to thank you for accommodating me last minute in the hotel," Douglas said.

"Yes, well you certainly made it worth our while," Maia said primly.

Douglas threw back his head and laughed, a loud, confident, male laugh that made her teeth clench.

"I'm sorry I'm leaving tomorrow," he said. "I would have liked to spend more time with you."

Maia didn't favor him with a response. She'd be happy to see the back end of the man. He had an unsettling way of viewing things, as if he saw far more than what was in front of him.

"Impressive little gig your grandfather put together," Callan continued, unperturbed by her coolness.

Maia sniffed. Was the man being deliberately obtuse? Afi might have the vision, but it took dozens more working behind the scene to ensure the festival's success.

She slid a sideways look toward Minerva. Her sister and that reporter had their heads angled together in what was obviously an intense exchange.

"Your grandfather invited Ryder and I to a shindig up at the hotel after the festival shuts down. Keep the party going."

Of course, he had. And failed to mention it to her, when she would be the one playing hostess and overseeing the staff. Maia huffed out a breath. It was difficult being the oldest, the responsible one in the family. The one everyone else counted on.

She tugged Minerva away from the reporter. "Come Minerva. Apparently, we have a party to prepare for."

"You go ahead. I'll be along shortly," Minerva said with a shy smile toward Ryder. "Mr. Lyon was just asking me about my art."

Maia sniffed again and turned on her heel. Had the entire world suddenly gone mad?

Selene watched the glowing sky as it grew brighter by the minute, lighting up the surrounding trees which grew thickly up the side of the mountain. Smoke hung heavily in the air, hiding the flames as they licked the roof of a derelict cabin tucked into the side of the mountain. If not for the fire marking its location, the structure would have been easy to overlook. The driver stopped a safe distance away. The well-trained horses stood their ground as the two men began unrolling the hose.

Selene climbed down, impressed with the way they went about doing their job. The river that fed Silver Spring Lake flowed nearby, likely why the cabin had been built here originally, near a fresh water source. Moments later she heard the sizzle as a stream of water reached the flames. She must be touched in the head, stowing away. What had she been thinking? What she ought to be doing was something useful, like looking for Beckett's whereabouts.

Careful to stand well back, she watched the two men extinguish the blaze before it spread further. Blackened timbers collapsed upon themselves. Before long, the entire structure wasn't much more than a smoldering mass of half-burned charcoal with only the back wall standing. Once the flames were doused, the firemen cautiously picked their way through the carnage. She tensed. Surely no one had been inside?

They emerged from the soggy mess moments later and began coiling up the hose. One of them paused as he passed her. "Lucky you spotted that when you did so we were able to contain it. Unchecked, it would have spread like crazy."

"A—any sign of anyone inside?" she said with forced casualness.

"Nope. Hard to know how the fire got started. Up here in the middle of nowhere. I thought maybe it got hit by a spark from the fireworks but they're too far away. Clem figures it must have been deliberate. He knows more about stuff like that."

"Deliberate?" Selene straightened. "As in someone was here recently?"

"That's what he figures."

While the men were busy securing their equipment, Selene made her way toward the burned ruins. Near what she assumed had originally been the entrance, her foot landed on something hard. The chunk of blackened metal had been singed, but mostly escaped the flames. She bent down and picked it up. A pocketknife. She brushed away the soot. Staring up at her were the initials BT.

She straightened and looked around. Her instincts hadn't failed her. Beckett had been here. She peered into the dark menacing woods surrounding the shack. But where was he now?

SQUATTING on the shoreline of the river, Beckett cupped handful after handful of clean, cold water to slake his thirst. It was black as Hades out here. Finally satisfied, he rocked back on his heels before he rose unsteadily to his feet. Whatever they'd drugged him with in Crawford's study was powerful stuff. His head still throbbed.

He straightened, thanking his knees for not buckling. His legs were stiff from the hours he'd spent wriggling on the dirt floor of the shack to finally free his knife from his pocket. It had taken some doing to open it and saw through his bonds without slicing his wrist open at the same time. Once free, he'd bunched up a roll of abandoned bedding from one corner of the shack, hoping that if Mathers checked, he'd see a shadowy lump and figure Beckett had just passed out again.

He needn't have bothered. From a nearby vantage point, he'd seen the pair ride up, set fire to the shack, and take off before he could even think about tackling them. Which wouldn't have been a smart move in his weakened state. Better to wait and catch them off guard. After all, they'd assume he'd gone up with the shack. Wouldn't they be surprised!

Once the pair had ridden away, he'd followed the sound of the river. Filtered moonlight through the trees showed him where the river bank widened enough that he could get a badly-needed drink. Refreshed, he started off. The river would lead him to the lake and the hotel.

BACK AT THE FIREHALL, on behalf of her grandfather, Selene thanked the two firemen for their efforts and left them tending the horses. The fireworks were over, signaling the official end to the festival, but High Street was still thronged with people. Her left hand clutched Beckett's knife as if it were some sort of talisman. A sign he hadn't perished in the fire, but had gotten away from his captors. She kept her right hand buried in her pocket close to her pistol, just in case.

No one paid her any mind as she moved through the crowd, searching for Bolton. She needed to show him Beckett's knife and explain where she had found it. How could she possibly spot anyone in this crowd? Outside the train station the clock struck midnight, yet it felt much later. As if she'd lived a lifetime in a single day. A lifetime without Beckett.

The clock! She raced toward the stately time piece that overlooked the town square and the station. She reached its base, grabbed hold of its ornate sidepieces and started to climb. It had been cleverly designed with a built-in ladder so the timekeeper could service it as needed, ensuring it kept the correct time. Halfway up she paused and looked down at those milling below.

Maybe Bolton was among the throng behind her, partway down the hill. She swiveled, then froze. Her heart leapt into her throat. Beckett strode toward her, larger than life, his gaze riveted on her.

He reached the clock, raised his arms and lifted her down. She threw her arms around him, laughing and crying at the same time, unable to speak. He looked tired and disheveled, and she had never seen a more wonderful sight.

Gently, he lowered her to the ground. "Where are Crawford and your sisters?"

CHAPTER 17

Beckett couldn't believe his eyes when he saw Selene clinging to the side of the clock stand. Relief at finding her safe immediately changed to alarm. She was a sitting duck for Mathers. And even though he wanted nothing more than to hold her forever, there were the others to consider. He had to reach them before Mathers.

He asked again, his voice urgent. "Where are Crawford and your sisters?"

"I don't know, I—"

"We have to warn them."

"About what? Who snatched you from Afi's study and took you to the abandoned shack?"

He didn't ask how she knew where he'd been held prisoner. That could wait.

"The Mathers. And from what they said, Crawford and you girls are their next targets."

"Why?"

He kept his arm tightly around her as he guided her through the crowd, scanning the faces of everyone they passed. "Mathers is Preston's half-brother, bound for revenge. He and Deirdre arrived first to case the place."

"How did he know about the tunnels? Beneath the hotel and leading to the emporium?"

"Apparently Preston knew Crawford well enough to know he would have an escape route in place. He bribed the architect and found out how to access the tunnel and where it came out at the other end."

"Oh, no!" Selene froze, then grabbed Beckett's hand and started to run. "Afi is hosting an end-of-festival party at the hotel. Mathers is bound to show up."

"Let's pray we get there first."

THEY ARRIVED to find the party going strong. Still holding her tight, Beckett wasted no time finding Crawford. Afi looked askance upon seeing them together, but listened intently as Beckett tersely relayed what he knew about the connection between Preston and Mathers. Afi summoned Bolton, and Beckett brought the other man up to speed on the Mathers and their connection to Preston.

Painful as it was to leave Beckett's side even for an instant, Selene went to find her sisters and warn them. Maia was in the formal dining room supervising Flo as that woman laid out some late-night refreshments. Her sister looked harried and distracted and it took a few minutes for Selene to not only get her attention, but to impress upon her the possible danger.

"But the Mathers checked out earlier," Maia said with a puzzled frown.

"That's what they want us to believe," Selene said.

"You don't think they'd try to pull something here, in front of all these witnesses, do you?"

"We don't know what they're planning," Selene said. "Where are the others?"

"I left Minerva talking to that reporter fellow. He seems keen on her idea to have artists showcase their work as part of next year's festival. She's hoping he'll write something that will reach artists across the country so they plan to attend."

Selene nodded, listening with half an ear. She continued to scan the arriving guests, watching for the Mathers. They could be in disguise.

Oh, lovely! In waltzed Adria as if she owned the place. Several young men and women that Selene hadn't seen before accompanied her.

Behind Adria, Callan Douglas filled the doorway. Selene noticed Maia quickly turned her back. She didn't blame her. She didn't trust the man, either. He was a little too smooth. Too affable. Too much everything. Afi said they went way back, but Selene knew Afi could be far too trusting.

And generous! For it appeared Afi had invited the entire town and all the festival participants, no doubt to entice them to take part next year and tell others. Before long, the hotel lobby was stretched to the seams. As more guests poured in, others spilled into the dining room, the games room and the parlor.

Near the grand piano, the older magician entertained onlookers with a card trick. Selene wondered where his sidekick was. And why was Chandra nowhere to be seen? What if she had been accosted by the Mathers?

Selene looked up to see a pair of clowns near the entrance. Her gaze skipped over them, then returned. There was something unsettling about the duo and the awkward way they moved in their oversize shoes. Across the room she saw Beckett make his way toward the clowns, edging behind the crowd in order to keep out of sight. What was he—?

No!

The taller clown popped the head off his cane and pulled out a rifle. No one else was paying attention, but Selene could see he had a clear shot across the lobby at Afi. When Beckett stepped up and tapped the clown on the shoulder he swung around, then froze.

Beckett wrestled the gun from the other man before he tore off the bright orange wig to reveal Mather's thinning gray hair. Bolton, meanwhile, had hold of the second clown who had lost her wig and hat when she attempted to flee. Deirdre Mathers scowled at her captor. Within seconds the two of them were escorted from the party by Beckett and Bolton.

Much as Selene longed to go after Beckett, she knew she could be more help here reassuring any nervous guests and downplaying what had just happened. Luckily, few had noticed anything amiss. Moments later, Beckett wove his way through the oblivious crowd to reach her side. She couldn't tear her eyes from him.

"I'm not sure if that was foolish or brave," she said. Her voice shook slightly in the aftermath of everything that had gone on this evening as Beckett gathered her close.

"I had the element of surprise on my side. The look on his face when he recognized me— At any rate, Bolton's handing those two over to sheriff Dodds. Apparently, he was here partaking of the festivities, and Bolton asked him to stick around in case something untoward went down."

"Is it really over?"

"Not quite," Beckett said. "But it will be soon. Your grandfather is making a beeline for us right now."

Selene looked up and smiled in relief. Afi was alive and well thanks to the speedy actions of Beckett. "He probably wants to thank you."

"Somehow, I doubt that's what he's coming to say."

Afi reached them and pointed to her, his eyes hard. "You. My study. Right this second."

Selene exchanged a look with Beckett, who raised his brow as if to say, 'I told you.'

Inside Afi's den, the door clicked shut behind her with an ominous sound. "What's this about closing down the emporium early?"

Selene stiffened, then faced her grandfather. "It was a decision made by Beckett and myself."

"Foolishness," Afi said. "Leaving good money on the table."

Selene was grateful not to have Beckett here. She needed to fight this one herself. "You didn't trust me from the start. You had no faith I could make the gaming hall a success."

"That's not entirely true. I hoped to save you from repeating some of the mistakes I made in my earlier days."

"You need to loosen the reins, Afi. On all of us. Let us figure things out our way. What worked before is not guaranteed to work in today's world."

"You sound like your grandmother," Afi said with a little smile. "She would have questioned my actions, the same way as you."

"Like forcing Beckett on me?"

"She would have come around eventually."

"You sound sure of that."

"I know you well, my dear. I had no guarantee when I set things in motion to have Beckett help lure Preston in for the kill. But I had my secret hopes."

"Beckett said you told him to stay away from me. That he

wasn't anyone you would welcome to the family. That he wasn't worthy."

"Blame that one on Beckett's father, not me. He's the one who filled the boy's head with nonsense about the pride of the south. That the family was worthless without its precious plantation. Beckett knows better of course, but sometimes it's hard to drown out those voices from our childhood."

"Minerva overheard you telling him he was nowhere near the kind of man to win my hand."

"Selene, the man is as stubborn as you are. Can you imagine if I said, 'Feel free to woo my granddaughter while you're here? I give you my blessing?' He would have lit out of here on the next train."

Selene didn't know if she should kiss him or slap him. "You conniving old so-and-so."

"I couldn't control the outcome, my dear. That had to come from your heart and Beckett's. But I did feel I had the blessing of dear Carolyn and your parents. That they would be as happy as me, should you and Beckett make a match."

"I'm tempted to reject him, just to thwart your matchmaking."

Afi smiled. "You're far too much of a romantic. I've seen the lustful way the two of you look at each other. It's enough to make an old man blush."

"Afi!"

"Don't forget. I was young once. And madly in love."

"Don't act too smug when he asks you for my hand."

"Don't worry. I shall act suitably gruff, and agree most reluctantly."

Selene eyed her grandfather admiringly. "I'm starting to see how you became such a success over the years. Dare I hope I inherited a little of that cunning?"

He laughed as he gave her a nudge. "Never mind that. Run along and tell Beckett I demand to speak to him. Don't let on what I just confided. Beckett is too proud to think he could fall for one of the oldest cons in the book."

"It'll be our little secret." She paused before she left. "I thought Bolton's job was to help find us all husbands."

Afi winked. "Eavesdroppers often hear what the other party wants them to hear."

Selene gasped. "You deliberately threw me off. While I was on guard against Bolton trying to introduce me to someone, you snuck Beckett in right under my nose."

Afi smiled fondly as he gave her a hug. "Don't tell your sisters."

"Why? Do you have suitors in mind for them as well?"

"Please. Let me walk one of you down the aisle before you start questioning my future motives."

Which didn't come close to answering her question.

Just then, he reached past her and opened the study door. "Ah, Beckett," he said. "Just the fellow I wanted to see. Please come in. Selene was just leaving."

SHE NEEDN'T HAVE WORRIED about keeping Afi's scheming ways from her sisters. They were too busy speculating about the Mathers.

"Surely they were the ones behind the jewelry thefts," Minerva said. "I mean they knew about the tunnels."

Selene didn't mention the obvious, that the thefts had begun long before the Mathers arrived. No point in ruining a relatively peaceful end to an evening that had more drama than any stage performance.

Luckily, no one noticed her distracted state as she

watched for Beckett to emerge from Afi's study. Around her, the conversation switched from the Mathers to the festival, and what the townsfolk might like to see happen next. She'd expected Beckett would see right through the old man's scheme, but when he joined her and her sisters a short time later, she wasn't so sure. Except for a few stragglers, the guests had finally left. The place was in total disarray, but Maia had shooed away the staff, telling them to leave the cleanup for the morning.

"The hotel guests will understand."

Could Maia be mellowing? Usually her sister obsessed over the hotel being perfect. Then she forgot about Maia and the others as Beckett swept her into his arms.

"It took some doing," he said. "But Crawford finally gave me his blessing."

"What's all this about?" asked Chandra.

"This." Selene pressed her lips to Beckett's in full view of everyone, which effectively put paid to their questions. Once they were quiet, she turned to them. "How do you three feel about being bridesmaids at our wedding?"

"As if you'd ask anyone else," Maia said. "Which one of us gets to be maid of honor?"

"All of you," Selene said, right before Beckett linked his fingers through hers and tugged her toward the balcony.

Before their eyes, dawn lightened the sky and the sun appeared from behind the mountains. She put one hand in her pocket and came out with his pocket knife. "I believe this belongs to you."

His jaw dropped as he took it from her and turned it over and over in his hand. "You found where they had taken me."

"You weren't getting away from me that easily.

Remember that in the future, should you decide to skip town."

"Never without you." They stood with their arms around her each other and her head tucked beneath his chin, watching in comfortable silence as a new day arrived. A new day to revel in their good fortune.

"I'm afraid we'll never get any privacy around here," Selene said.

"In that case, we should get married as soon as possible. Crawford's promised to build us a house in town."

"I hope you told him that we'll build our own home, to our own tastes."

"I did," Beckett said, a smile tugging at his lips. "But I generously allowed him to bequeath us the property for it from his many holdings."

"Good," Selene said, turning in his arms to face him. She tilted her head toward his. "Afi needs to learn he can't always get things his way."

"I couldn't agree more." Their kiss sealed a promise for here and for now, for their future and the future of Silver Springs Junction.

Watch for Chandra's story, *The Magician*, Book 2 of *The Spinster Takes a Groom* to release summer 2024.

AFTERWORD

Thanks for reading *The Gambler*. You might not know how important reader reviews are, but they mean a lot.

Review wherever you purchased *The Gambler* or on Goodreads or BookBub.

Just a short sentence saying you enjoyed the book goes a long way with new readers and puts a smile on this author's face.

And please keep in touch

Website: www.KathleenLawless.com
Facebook: facebook.com/kathleenlawlessnovels
Instagram: instagram.com/kathleenflawless
TikTok: tiktok.com/@kathleenflawless

Sign up for my VIP reader newsletter to receive updates, special giveaways and fan-priced offers. http://eepurl.com/bVosb1

Hope

Janie

Sweet Western Historical Romance

MAIL ORDER BRIDES

Mail Order Olivia

Mail Order Rachel

Mail Order Martina

A Bride for Shane

A Bride for Riley

A Bride for Weston

Mail Order Noelle

Chelsea's Choice

Lila: Rescue Me Mail Order Brides

Here Come the Brides Volume 1

Here Come the Brides Volume 2

Sweet Contemporary Romance

Frannie (Always a Bridesmaid)

Baxter (Last Man Standing)

Blue Sky Island

One Cinderella Spring

One Stolen Summer

One Fantasy Fall

One Wondrous Winter

Sweet Christmas Romance Novellas

Holly's Wish

No Groom at the Inn

Women's Fiction

Fabulous at Fifty

Romantic Suspense

Final Heat

Afterburn

Steamy Historical Romance

Taboo

Unmasked

Reckless Rogues - Box Set of the 2 Books

Steamy Contemporary Romance

SECRET SEDUCTIONS

Her Untamed Cowboy - Book 1

Her Undercover Cowboy - Book 2

Her Unwilling Cowboy - Book 3

Who Needs a Cowboy! - Book 4

Intimate Strangers

For a complete book list visit KathleenLawless.com

To be the first to hear about Kathleen's new releases, special fan pricing sales, and also receive a free book, sign up for her VIP Reader Newsletter at http://eepurl.com/bV0sb1

ABOUT THE AUTHOR

USA Today Bestselling Author, Kathleen Lawless, blames a misspent youth watching Rawhide, Maverick and Bonanza for her fascination with cowboys, which doesn't stop her from creating a wide variety of interests and occupations for her many alpha male heroes.

With over 50 published novels to her credit, she enjoys pushing the boundaries of traditional romance into historical romance, contemporary romance, romantic suspense and women's fiction.

She makes her home in the Pacific Northwest and loves to hear from her readers.

Sign up for Kathleen's VIP Reader Newsletter to receive updates, special giveaways and fan-priced offers. http://eepurl.com/bVosb1

KathleenLawless.com

goodreads.com/kathleenlawless
bookbub.com/authors/kathleen-lawless
facebook.com/kathleenlawlessnovels
instagram.com/kathleenflawless
tiktok.com/@kathleenflawless